Www.LarryRedmond.Com

The
Reward
of the
Fool

The Reward of the Fool
by
Larry Redmond

Penknife Press   Chicago, Illinois

This is a work of fiction. The characters, dialogue and events described herein are the products of the author's imagination, and do not portray actual persons or events.

Resentment kills a fool, and envy slays the simple.

The Holy Bible
Job 5:2

. . . because I will reward you handsomely and do whatever you say.
Come and put a curse on these people for me..

The Holy Bible
Numbers 22:17

My life has been wasted. Squandered. Thrown away like a bag of shit. And I'm the one who did it. Second by second, breath by breath, I spent it. I spent it a penny at a time, penny after penny after penny.

It's a funny thing about pennies. They don't seem worth much. So they're easy to throw around. At first, they don't appear to be the atoms, molecules, cells of a life. So you throw them away without really thinking about it. Sometimes one at a time, sometimes by the fistful. The other thing about pennies is that they disappear quickly. They don't hang around under your feet reminding you that they've just been thrown away. So you forget. Then one day after several decades of watching them fly from your hand in a steady stream, your reach into the theretofore bottomless bag for yet another handful, and you feel it. You feel the sides of the canvas bag rubbing ever so lightly against the knuckles at the back of your hand. It happened to me for the first time this morning.

I guess the notion to stop and take stock wasn't new. It had insinuated itself into my mind countless times over the years. Always uninvited, always quickly dispatched. But *this* morning was different. *This* morning, I felt the sides of the canvas bag against my knuckles. *This* morning, I wanted to see exactly what my pennies had purchased.

I made a list. I actually got a pen and ink and some paper, and I wrote it down. I wrote 'MY LIFE' in capital letters across the top of the first sheet of a stack about a quarter inch thick of clean, white, acid-free, 25% cotton fibre, 24 pound bond. Each sheet had the manufacturer's watermark emblazoned in the middle, a round circle with a winged dragon clutching a ribbon banner with the manufacturer's name in calligraphic script. I wrote clear, blue Arabic numerals along the lefthand margin careful to ensure that the period after each one was spaced a consistent distance from the numeral itself. This was going to be a document that I could frame and hang on the wall and point to and say with some degree of justifiable pride, "This is my life."

I pondered the first entry. The words, 'I was born' leapt to mind quickly followed by a date: a month, a day, a year. Then I thought about it. There was nothing especial about that month, that day, that year. Hundreds, indeed thousands, of people could make the exact same claim. Everybody ever born could at least make a similar claim. No, that wasn't the kind of first entry I wanted. I wanted something bold, something that would stand out, make someone take notice.

This time, the words 'I graduated' came to me quickly followed by the names of schools I had attended. Admiral David Glasgow Farragut High School and Wilson Junior College. But again, so what? Hundreds, thousands, hundreds of thousands could make the same claim, or even better ones.

The thought that I had been in the military made me chuckle.

I stared at the numeral one and the little period that followed it. Then it struck me. I hadn't done anything worthy of note. I was nothing. I was no one. I had made no mark. Shit!

I had just recently arrived at Chicago's O'Hare Airport from a job in Texas. I had just killed a man. That's what I am. That's what I do. His name was Avel. His name is always Avel. I killed him to stop him from killing America. I killed him for the good of democracy.

What his real name was isn't important. It's what he did that counts. What he did was head up Post, Tanne and Leef, the construction company that made billions of dollars over the years supporting U.S.

military aggression around the world. He didn't just support military aggression, he contributed to the campaigns of politicians who advocated for war, who sought war. In fact, he ran for president himself. He and people like him start wars just so their corporations can make money. He thinks the president should be above the law. He thinks that *all* rich people should be above the law. He thinks its okay for poor people's blood to run in the streets. His favorite line during his campaign was that he had no quarrel with the people of whatever country he wanted to invade, only their leaders. Never mind that it is the people with whom he has no quarrel that end up dying by the hundreds of thousands. Almost every war this country has been in since World War II was started with those words.

Well, today he got his comeuppance. Today, *I* was above the law.

It was easy. From a distance, I reconnoitered his every move. As a candidate, he had had the Secret Service watching over him. But the election was over, and he lost, so they were gone. I'm partial to poisons, so I was looking for a way to get him with nicotine. It took about a month, but I noticed that he liked toothpicks. He always had one close by. From what I could see, he had a hole of some kind– a cavity, a gap– around his upper right molars. After every meal, he would get his toothpick, and pry out stuck food.

I knew how I wanted to kill him, but I wasn't sure I'd be able to pull it off. I began to conduct a reconnaissance of his house. He lived in a mansion. It didn't have guards, but it had a camera system with motion detectors connected to lights to record everything that happened on the grounds and around the house. It did not, however, have people monitoring the system 24/seven. I knew that a black ninja suit with FBI markings would do the trick, but I still wasn't sure about how to deliver the hit. That's when I got lucky. I found a dead blowfish on the beach. It wasn't as big as they come, only about eight inches long, but I felt like I had struck gold. I kept heavy gloves in the car, and I used them to carry this baby back to the car and back to the hotel where I was staying. I bottled as much of its fluids as I could salvage, and disposed of the rest.

I didn't know what kind of toothpicks Avel used, so I got an assortment. I soaked three of each in the blowfish fluid, dried them, and stashed them in a plastic bag.

The motion sensors were placed at the sides of the house, and in the back. So, dressed in my FBI black ninja suit, I ran straight up to the front door at 3:00 o'clock in the morning. I used a bump key to open the front door, and headed for the kitchen. I wore soft kung-fu boots, and hugged the walls as I moved to lessen the chance of the floors squeaking. I used a weightless technique I had learned years earlier from my teacher. I found his toothpick box. He liked the flat ones. I took the flat ones from my plastic bag, and put them in his box right on top. Then I left the way I came in.

Back at the hotel, I pondered how long I should wait around town to make sure the job was done. But the lead story on the noon news the next day made the decision easy.

"This just in," the broadcaster said, "the CEO of Post, Tanne and Leef was found dead this morning on his kitchen floor. The cause of death is unknown. Police are investigating."

That was all I needed. I packed up, and headed for the airport.

The flight was late arriving, and I was tired. The taxi dispatcher waved me to a dented, red and white Ford. One of the bulbs in the taxi's beacon was out. I threw my bag onto the rear seat and crawled in behind it. My butt slid into the depression that had been created by countless other passengers' butts. The car was cold, smelled of gasoline, and had standing water on the floor behind the driver. I didn't care. I just wanted to get home.

"Welcome to La Guardia!" the driver shouted in a thick New York accent. He slapped the top of the dashboard to get the instrument panel to work.

La Guardia?! Did I take the wrong plane? Have I been somnambulating for the last twenty minutes? I sat up straight and looked around for clues. This *looked* like O'Hare.

The driver was a big man, about 30 years old with pock marks on his cheeks from teenage acne. His head was covered with dark curly locks, and he steered over a sizeable beer belly.

I told him this was Chicago.

"New York is a great town," he bellowed. "I'm shore you'll enjoy your visit." He stomped on the gas so that the corner of his cab could establish a place in traffic, then stomped on the brake because there was no place to go.

I told him again this was Chicago.

"New York! Chicago! They're all the same," he said.

A ten foot interval opened up in traffic. He lurched into it, then jammed the brake.

"Where you goin'?" he asked.

I gave him the address.

"Oh, yeah," he said, "Sheridan Road. That's way on the west side of town."

I was beginning to catch on. Sheridan Road was east by the lake.

"Just so you know," he said, "the trip will be between 18 and 22 dollars."

He was right. I usually spent 20 dollars for this ride, and that included a generous tip. I looked over at the meter and saw that a thick cable dangled loose out of one side of it.

A small clearing opened up in traffic. He leaned on the horn, then leaned on the gas. He peeled around an airport bus, then stopped short behind a string of other cabs. He tapped the horn again, this time to get the attention of a black porter beside whom we happened to have stopped. They exchanged waves and greetings that I couldn't hear above the roar of traffic. Another clearing opened up, and we zoomed through a small space between a black Cadillac limousine and a short, silver limousine bus. There was about a foot of clearance on each side. Then, like magic, we were on the open road, the I190 home.

I sat back and watched the signs and lights and passing traffic. "Welcome to Chicago, Richard M. Daley, Mayor." Cities are beautiful places at night. Everything is lights. Red taillights. Yellow signal lights. Blue, green and white lights framing and topping the buildings of the downtown. There is something comforting about seeing familiar surroundings. I began to relax in a way that I hadn't been able to for days, especially since this morning. I began to anticipate being in my own apartment, my own bathroom, my own shower, my own bed.

Oddly, the gasoline smell pulled me back to the musings of earlier in the day. As is my wont, I contemplated death immediately prior to my flight. Is that what people in airports think about? Everybody knows that few have survived airplane crashes. Do we all do it? Calculate the odds? The chances? Recall the statistic comparing airplane deaths to automobile deaths? How many people *do* die in car accidents per miles traveled anyway? How many miles are traveled by car? Does anybody know? How many people die because of gasoline fumes in cabs?

If I were to die today, now, what would I regret not having done? What is the fulfilled life anyway? What does it mean? Who has it, and who missed out?

The road between O'Hare and Chicago is right under one of the approach lanes to the airport. I watched the planes high in the distance bank into the lane, and follow one behind the other to the runway every thirty seconds or so. The pitch of the roar increased until they were directly overhead, then decreased as they each disappeared into the lights of traffic out the back window.

On balance, my life was good. Maybe more than on balance. Maybe by any measure, my life was good. I had not made the money I always thought I would, but now I knew that was a plus. In this country, men are measured by many yardsticks. How much can you drink and smoke? How many women have you laid? How big is your dick? Greatest among them is, how much money have you made?

There was no question about it, money was power. Look rich, and people will treat you altogether differently. I remembered going to the Boat and Camping Show at McCormick Place some years ago. I and my woman *du jour* were in line to tour a yacht. I had on my long hair beaver coat. I had just recently declared bankruptcy, but never mind that. We looked the part.

The people showing the boat looked bored until we stepped on. My woman was wearing a full-length tanuki. The ship came to life. People began to minister to us. I told them straight away that I could not afford a boat. No matter. They told me that I might one day. They showed us every inch of the place.

But it wasn't real. They weren't reacting to me. They were reacting to whom they thought I was. Worse, they were reacting to whom they thought I might become.

The cab pulled into the semicircle driveway in front of my building. The light from the vestibule provided enough light for me to count my money out.

"Twenty bucks," he said, "and don't forget to catch a show on Broadway."

"That's low for New York," I said. "Here's twenty-five."

I was still tired, but I felt strangely refreshed. I opened the door, and wiggled out of the dented seat pulling my bag behind me. The driver flipped me a smile and a wink. "My man," he said, then stomped on the gas, and lurched out into the traffic. I placed my back against the glass vestibule door, and pushed my way inside.

I checked my mail, then let myself in the inside security door. As I pushed the elevator button, I looked at myself in the mirrored hallway. I was different now. What happened to that young boy whose school pictures I used to be so ashamed of? How did his skin get so weathered looking, his hair so grey? Black might not crack, but it sure as hell will sag. I studied my image. The curve of my pointed chin and shallow cheek bones, the full lips and bony, angular nose were the same as they were when I was young, but the lips had parentheses around them now. The close set, light brown eyes were more heavily pigmented, and had bags under them. The widow's peak was gone, pushed away by the swath of shiny skin on the top of my head that defined the horseshoe shape of the hair around the outside of my head. Not only had my life been squandered, now I was ugly.

When the elevator door opened, I stepped in eagerly hoping against hope that the image I had been studying would remain behind.

It's the choices we make that determine who we are. So what was wrong with my choices?

I remembered the day I got shot. I was at Rainbow Beach, lying under a cottonwood tree. I saw this Chinese woman wearing a purple silk Manchurian jacket duck to the ground. She had heard shots before, and knew what to do. She was about twenty-eight, and the ends of her waist-length silky black hair waved in the breeze as she moved. Her dark almond eyes darted from side to side. Her delicate round and flat face was calm. She saw the assassin leave, then, crouching low, ran to help me. She made no sound as she moved.

I was surprised that I opened my eyes. It felt like Sunday. It felt like Easter Sunday. I had expected to be dead. In fact, I was dead. Al Pearsons no longer lived. That single shot set him free. Now, all I had to do was live. Who was I going to be? A corollary to the ontological question of all times: Who am I? I was no longer Noel Bodie, and Al Pearsons was dead. I knew I would never die. Who would I be?

The young Chinese woman had her mouth on my mouth, blowing her life into my lungs. Feeling the pain in my side, I flinched. The woman raised up and looked at me. She seemed pleasantly surprised to see me.

"Don't die," she said. "Don't die. I'll call a doctor."

"No doctor," I said. "No doctor."

"You need a doctor!"

"It's okay if I die. I don't want a doctor."

I reached over and felt the clump of rags she had wedged at my side to stanch the flow of blood. She had used the jacket she had been wearing. "How bad is it?" I asked.

"I don't know," she said. "There are two holes, one in front and one in the back. You're bleeding from both of them."

"Good. It went through. Is the blood oozing out, or is it pumping out?"

"It's oozing. What does that mean?"

"What's your name?"

"Jiqin Dong."

"I need you to help me home, Jiqin."

"I'm taking you to a doctor."

"No doctor!"

"I'm taking you to my uncle's place."

"No, Jiqin, please. No one must know."

"What is *your* name?"

I had to think fast. Jesus, what was I going to say? The Lord's name teased my lips, "Je . . . Jes . . .."

"Jay?" she asked.

"Yeah," I answered, "Jay."

"My uncle will take care of you, Jay. He's a doctor."

I couldn't let her take me to a doctor. Doctors are required to report gunshot wounds to the police. If this wound got reported, the wrong people might find out about it.

"You got a last name, Jay?"

Still holding the wad of rags, I swung a back fist at her head with my right hand. She blocked it easily. I scarcely felt her touch on my wrist.

"What your last name?"

"I'm just a guy," I answered, "you don't know me." I swung at her with my left hand. Using the same hand, she blocked that, too.

"Stop fighting me, Jay Guy. I try to help you," she said. "What your middle name?"

By then, I had thought of a good first name. "Samuel," I said. I didn't know why I picked Samuel. I couldn't remember having ever known anyone who called himself Samuel.

"Jay Sam Guy," she said.

"Yeah," I answered. "Just some guy." Then I fainted.

I didn't remember the trip to her uncle's house. I just remembered opening my eyes and seeing Jiqin and an old Chinese man that looked like he could have stepped out of a Fu Manchu Mystery. He was tiny. He was old. He smelled of herbs that I didn't recognize. There was a naked light bulb. I was hot and I was freezing. I shivered under the blankets they had on me. My breathing was shallow because it hurt to take deep breaths. I felt the room begin to spin. I heard the roar of mosquitoes buzzing in both ears. My eyes closed by themselves.

My eyes opened by themselves, like a doll's eyes when you sit her upright. I was staring at the ceiling. The room was light even though the naked bulb is off. Almost as an exercise, I moved my eyes from one side to the other, from one object to the other, from the lightbulb to the single strand of spider web hanging from the ceiling in the corner, to the cream painted wood molding going around the wall at the ceiling, to the small round window at the top of the wall to my right, to the crack in the wall that had been repaired with plaster that was itself cracking again in the exact same place. I turned my head slowly and followed the crack down to the walnut table resting beside the wall. There was a glass pitcher filled with water on the table. There was an empty glass.

This didn't look like a hospital. I tightened my stomach muscles in order to sit up, and felt the pain. I let out a short moan. Within less than a minute, the door to my left opened up, and Jiqin Dong looked in. She wore a tattered grey University of Wisconsin t-shirt and a long denim skirt.

"Jay," she said. "You didn't die."

I was about to look around to see who Jay was, then I remembered that was my new name. "Where am I?"

"You woke up just in time," she said pouring water into the glass.

"Help me up."

"We have to leave town." She helped me sit up.

"Why? What's up?" I sipped some water.

Before she could answer, there was a loud pounding at a door that sounded like it was downstairs.

Jiqin panicked. "They here!"

"Who's here?" I asked.

"The INS is after my uncle. He sneaked into the country three months ago in a cargo container with some other people. They want to deport him."

The INS pounded on the door again. "Open up in there," someone said.

"Pretend this is your house." She begged, "please."

I could hear a small glass pane being broken, then the door being unlocked, and being flung open and hitting hard against the wall. I could hear heavy footfalls on the floor below me. It sounded like a football team running through the house. Finally, there were heavy feet thumping up the stairs outside my room. The door crashed open and three men lunged in, falling over themselves. They were dressed in cheap, ill-fitting suits, one grey, one blue, one brown. The one in grey was tall; his suit was too short. The one in blue was fat; his suit was too snug. The one in brown was small; his suit was baggy. They looked at me, and stopped in their tracks.

"Who's going to fix that glass?" I asked.

"Who the fuck are you?" the tall one asked back.

"I own this place."

"We thought she owned it," he said, gesturing to Jiqin.

"Would it be all right to break into the house without a warrant if she owned it?" I asked.

"We have a warrant."

"Let's see it."

"Okay, we don't have a warrant."

"Then get the fuck out."

"We'll be back later."

"Bring some money for that window," I said.

As they left, they broke the rest of the windows in the door. Why do cops always do shit like that?

I lived in an abandoned apartment building on Seventy-seventh and Lakeshore Drive by Rainbow Park. I found it years ago when I got back from a trip to Europe. It was from there that I had created the character of Al Pearsons. It was there that Ida and I returned after striking a blow for freedom. There is where she went crazy.

It was a three-flat in which a fire had gutted the first floor. The back porch was still in tact, though, and the third floor was surprisingly clean. All of it, that is, except the kitchen. The kitchens on all three floors were destroyed. I slept in the master bedroom on the third floor huddled against the closed door so that no one would walk in on me undetected.

I left and reentered the house only after dark through a basement window. I didn't want anyone to know that the house was being used. I even rearranged the rubble at both entrances to discourage anyone from exploring. It was perfect! I felt like Ellison's invisible man. No one knew I was there, and yet I had all the comforts of a paid-for apartment. The water was still on, and one outlet in the building still worked. It was located in the basement behind the furnace, but it didn't appear to draw juice from the building's circuits. I never did figure out why. I used a series of extension cords to provide power to my room on the top floor. A space heater and hot plate provided me with heat and warm beverages throughout the winter. I didn't know why the building remained empty all this time.

I told Jiqin that she and her uncle could stay with me. I gave them the ground rules. Come and go only after dark. Stay away from the windows. No loud noises.

After about a week there, Jiqin suggested that we didn't have to hide.

"I checked it out," she said. "The owner of this building lives somewhere in Mississippi."

"What's your point?" I asked.

"The neighbors won't know that we're not the new owners. We can simply open the place up, make a few repairs, have the light and gas turned on, and live here."

"No," I said.

"Why not?"

"Because I said no."

"That's not good enough." She turned to walk out.

"What about the INS?" I asked.

"They have no clue where we are," she said on her way down the stairs.

The girl was stupid. Of course the INS had no clue where they were. But if she wanted to keep it that way, they would have to keep a low profile. I tried to raise up to argue my point before she got out of earshot, but a wave of pain in my side stopped me. I flopped back down on my mat, and clenched my teeth.

Then I thought about it. I wasn't the one in danger here. Nobody was looking for me. They all thought I was dead. That thought was my only comfort in the days and weeks that followed. I decided not to oppose the project.

I don't know where she found them, but she managed to get a crew of half a dozen guys together to work on the place. One of them was her uncle. But the others, I had never seen before. They were all Chinese; they were all illegal. They spoke no English, but they worked. They cleaned the debris from in front of the doors. They fixed and cleaned all the windows. They fixed the kitchens on all three floors. It wasn't like new, but it was sound, and it was weather tight. Jiqin shouted orders like a drill sergeant, all in Chinese. Even her uncle obeyed her every command.

The men rarely came up to the third floor, but when they did, they would bow to me. It wasn't a deep bow, just a slight bending at the waist and a lowering of the head and eyes. Especially her uncle. I figured it was because he felt he owed me, but he seemed to go out of his way to bow to me. I asked Jiqin what that was all about.

"I told them this your house," she said. "I told them I represent you, and if they don't do as I say, you will have them deported, or worse, killed."

"You told them *what*?!"

"Don't worry," she said, "I take care of everything."

"Who's paying for all of this?"

"They work for free," she answered.

"And the supplies?"

"Don't worry," she said, "police won't come after *you*."

I got the real answer after the work was done. The guys who did the work moved in the following day. They moved in on the second floor, all of them except the uncle. They all found someplace to go during the day, but by evening, they were all there studying English or reading Chinese newspapers. They did nothing to draw attention to themselves.

By then, my wound was healed enough that I could move around with some degree of ease. I felt as if I were on vacation. I didn't have to hide anymore. What would I do with myself? Who might I become? Better yet, who was I now? Shakespeare asked it first. What's in a name? Mine, this time, was Jay. But so what? Wherefore art thou Jay? Thou art Jay because thou christened thyself Jay. But again, so what? I answered to Jay, but I was who I was. Would Jay by any other name be as devoid of direction? Would Jay as Oliver still be Jay? Would Oliver as Jay? Oliver Nelson? Eddie Oliver?

Living in the streets, out of mainstream society, below the radar for years can warp a man if he isn't warped already. I had lived– hidden is a better word-- in this house for longer than I cared to remember. I was a young man when I began hiding out. By then, I was nearly middle-aged, and all I had to show for it was the fact that I was still breathing. Well, no. I had more. I had my freedom. I had my freedom, and I had my writings. But having the house remodeled even a little gave me an eerie feeling. It marked the end of an epoch.

Part of the change in no small measure was the fact that I lived with someone now. My life in the street was a solitary existence. It had to be, because I couldn't trust anyone. But then I lived with this woman and her uncle. We weren't exactly cohabiting– they had their part of the apartment; I had mine– but they were there. More to the point, *she* was there.

I hadn't been with a woman since Ida left, haunted by and running from the images of death she had helped create. I should never have let Ida come with me that night. She was no killer, but there was no way to know that. There was no way to know that night that I *was* a killer. Ida's ghost was that she had killed someone. My ghost, the one that I had been carrying around concealed in my breast all those years like one might carry the corpse of a mouse whose stench one would have to struggle to conceal, was that I wanted to do it again. I was ashamed to look at it. Its smell sickened me. But when Jiqin mentioned that she had told her workers that I might kill them, my reaction was: *what?* But my *gut* reaction was: *yes! Let's do it again!*

I asked Jiqin if she and her uncle wouldn't be more comfortable on the first floor by themselves. She smiled a little smile, and looked at the floor. She looked like one of the guys downstairs looking at the floor as they bowed.

"You protected us," she said, "and my uncle feels that we owe you. Part of the reason we fix your house is because we owe you."

"It's not my house," I said.

"To him, it is your house."

"You owe me nothing."

"If you had not saved him from the INS," she said, "he would have been deported back to China, and maybe killed. He owes you everything."

"Well, we're even," I said. "He saved my life before I saved his."

"There is one other small thing," she said, looking at the floor again. "Here we are your guests, and we might need your protection again."

"You would be my guests on the first floor as well."

"We were hoping to bring other guests there." Now she was almost bowing like the guys downstairs.

"Who?" I asked.

"Mexican guests," she said.

"Mexicans?!"

"They have money," she said. "Their money paid for food and these repairs."

"Fuckin' Mexicans?! Are you smugglers?!" The mere thought was exciting.

"Liberators," she said.

"These people are getting robbed and killed by smugglers."

"Yes," she said. "In the wrong hands, they are in danger. In our hands, they get treated fairly."

"Why are you telling me this?"

"We need a house."

"How do you know I can be trusted?"

"A man who gets shot and who does not want a doctor can be trusted. Besides," she said, "I know you."

Maybe this was it, the new me. "What's in it for me?" I asked.

"What do you want?" she asked back.

I couldn't help myself. It's almost as if my eyes moved of their own volition. Against my will, I began staring at her chest. She really didn't have any tits to speak of. They were more like over-sized nipples. And in the baggy t-shirt she wore, they were barely visible. But I couldn't look away.

"You want sex?" she asked.

"Yes," I said, "no!" Then I said yes again, then I said no again.

Then I tried to act as if I really meant it. I turned my back on her. "No," I said, "not like this."

"Then, how?"

"I don't want your pity."

"I'm not cute enough?" she asked.

"You're cute enough."

"My chest not big enough?"

"It's big enough."

"Then why you not want sex?"

"I *do* want sex."

"Okay, let's do it."

"I want love," I said. I sounded like a fool even to myself.

"Love?" She said, "This is business. I have something you want; you have something I want. Just business."

"Let's talk about it tomorrow," I said.

"The Mexicans will be here tomorrow," she said. "We need a deal tonight."

"I need to think a few minutes," I said.

"Okay," she said. "I go wash myself."

I could hear her turn to leave, and I turned to watch her. From behind, she looked like a boy, skinny with no ass. At the last minute before reaching the door, she turned her head and caught me looking at her butt. Her tiny mouth hinted at a smile.

Choices. Maybe I shouldn't have let Jiqin and her uncle stay. I stepped off the elevator when it arrived at my floor. The image in the panel of mirrors across from the elevator was the same, so I looked away. God, I hated my appearance.

I unlocked my door and went inside. The room smelled of

sandalwood and linseed oil. I flipped the light switch. I was finally home. No mirrors, no funky images. Just my stuff. My books. My swords on the walls. My drapes. My black leather couch. My aquarium. I plugged the aquarium light back into the timer, and the little guys darted back and forth. I kept African cichlids, about a dozen of them in a 55 gallon tank. Blue, golden yellow, orange. They looked African, big lips and eyes. They looked like me, and they were glad to see me. They knew they were about to be fed. I kept smelts in the freezer for them. I took a few out and ran water on them to thaw them. When I opened the lid, the little guys went wild, leaping to get the first bite. Water splashed all over me. I dropped the smelts in, and the guys attacked, snatching pieces off. I loved watching them eat. There was something about the colors and the light and the plants and frankly the carnage that calmed me. The blue one, the only blue one in the tank, was bigger than the others. I called him Chuck. Chuck ran the tank. Or at least he tried to. He snatched a mouthful of a smelt that was as big as he was, then tried to shoo the others away. Like he could eat the whole damn thing! He acted like an idiot. The other cichlids gave him his props. He was, after all, bigger than any of them. But they just circled around his posturing, and snatched more food. Chuck was the blue number one, but in the end, the little guys always won.

II

"Why did you help me?" I had to ask that question in order to forestall her asking the how-was-it question. I didn't want her to ask, because I didn't want to have to lie. She was the worst fuck I had ever had in my life. It's not that I had had that many women in my life. In truth, I had only had a few. But Jiqin Dong had no clue what to do with a man.

"You hurt me," she said. She was lying there huddled on her edge of the pallet in the fetal position. "I a virgin, and you hurt me." There was a pout in her tone of voice.

"A virgin?" I said, "I'm sorry." Maybe I was a little rough with her. "I didn't know. You were so . . ." My voice trailed off. I wanted to say brazen, brassy, forward. But then I thought that might add insult to injury. I felt ashamed. I felt like an animal. Reflecting back on it, I devoured her. She was the first woman I had had in ten years, and I couldn't stop myself. I was like a pile driving machine.

This time I asked to forestall her asking the how-could-you-do-that-to-me question. "So, why *did* you help me?"

"I don't know why," she said. Her voice was more relaxed for a moment. Then it got that edge again. "I wish I let you die."

"Look," I said, "I'm really sorry." I put my hand on her bony hip. She shifted away from my touch. "I didn't know," I said. "The way you came on, so direct, so matter-of-fact, I thought you were more experienced."

"I didn't want you to think I a little girl," she said.

"Next time I'll be gentle," I said. I put my hand on her shoulder, and she gave a little shrug. I scooched down behind her and into the spoon position. I slipped my hand over her waist, and rubbed her stomach. "It not so bad," she said. "It feel better."

We lay there long enough that I began to doze, and she twitched in my arms because she was dozing, too.

We didn't screw any more that day. In fact, we didn't screw again for another week. But we slept together every night. It was rough. I slept naked. And every night, I could smell her there next to me. She slept in a t-shirt and her panties. The first night, I spooned with her. I wanted to, but I didn't dare feel her up. The shame of that first session was still strong. I woke up the following morning with my dick as hard as a broom stick. After that, I stayed on my side of the bed. About a week passed before she came to bed naked, too.

"I help you," she said, "because you look like the Buddha."

"What?" I asked.

"I help you because you look like the Buddha," she said again. "You look like a picture my mother had next to the Buddha at home."

I had never noticed it before, but her voice was tiny, like a child's voice. And I was surprised that her words, those tiny baby words, had such a profound effect on me. I caught my breath. I literally stopped breathing remembering how years before, Lillian, an old woman in Germany that I met while stationed there in the Air Force, had told me that I looked like God. She meant that I looked like my Great Uncle Buddy King with whom she had been in love during World War I, and who had been the founder of a religious group the head of which, according to Lillian, I was the heir apparent. The remembrance of Lillian brought a flood of images to my mind. I remembered the car crash in the German woods after she strangled Hans, her driver, to death. Hans had learned who she believed I was, and was bent on revealing my whereabouts to a rival group bent on assassinating me. I remembered that I was the last living member of the King family. I wondered how my life would have turned out had I gone with her to Stockholm as Lillian had wanted instead of coming back to the States. What if I had become the Messiah they believed I was. I certainly would have had a lot more pussy over the last ten years.

I was already huddled on my side of the bed curled into a ball. I straightened out a little. I forced myself to breathe again, and I relaxed a little. "Yes," I said, "the Buddha."

"She said that she was one of your children."

"Seine Kinder," I said.

"Yes!" she said. "You know them?"

"I've heard of them," I said.

"Well, that's why I help you," she said. "You look like that picture."

"We all look alike," I said.

"Yeah," she said. "You do." There was wonderment in her voice. This time, she spooned behind me, and put one leg over my waist. I ignored her. After being shot, I was so relieved at the idea that folks now thought that I was dead that it never crossed my mind to wonder how they found me in the first place. Was it luck? Or could someone have led them to me that day by the beach? And how did that someone find me? How would that someone even know me? Jiqin pressed herself against my butt. I guess she wasn't having any of this ignore-her madness.

"Are you sure about this?" I asked.

"I sure," she said. She reached around and squeezed my dick. "It so big." There was that wonderment again.

I smiled to myself. This girl had never seen a really big dick. I wasn't all that big, but I seemed big to her because she was so small. "Yeah," I chuckled, "I know it's big." I rolled over onto my back feeling alternately like Superman and a phony. After about three seconds, the Superman feeling won out.

"What I do?" she asked.

Not wanting to risk losing control and doing the pile driver thing again, I said, "Sit up, and crawl on top of me."

She did. She drew her knees up so that she was astride my body, and relaxed so that I could enter her more easily. But it only helped a little. She was simply too small. She was gallant and endured the pain as best she could, but when tears began to well up in her eyes, I moved to take it out.

"No," she said, "leave it in. I a woman now. I will get bigger."

So I left it in. We fell asleep with her lying on top of me like a rag doll nailed to a board, and with me feeling like the biggest jerk in the world.

She woke me up by whispering in my ear. "They here," she said.

"The Mexicans? Here? Now?" I sat up abruptly. Jiqin was already dressed. I looked out of the window. It was still dark.

"Yes," she said. "They early."

I could hear the diesel engine of a large truck idling in the alley. "How many people are here?" I asked.

"23," she said.

"23 people?! Where are we going to put them?"

"In the downstair apartment," she said.

"No," I said, "it's too small."

"They'll be fine," she insisted.

So we moved them in, nine women and fourteen men. It was a real zoo. I didn't know how long they had been in that trailer, but they smelled like shit, literally. The driver paid Jiqin $500 a piece, $11,500 in cash. He was a little man with a huge beer belly. In front of the truck, out of sight of his passengers, he peeled off hundred dollar bills by the score. Then he climbed back into his cab. The air reeked of diesel smoke for several minutes after he drove away.

Once inside, they all crowded noiselessly into the livingroom. It was as if being stacked on top of each other had become normal for them. The familiar feel and smell of the next person's body was somehow comforting. The room was thick with cumin and funk.

"Welcome to America," Jiqin said.

There was a pause. Then a smile began to spread across one woman's face, then another, then a man's. Within a few seconds, the entire room was animated with grinning faces and staccato chatter in Spanish.

"Shhhh," Jiqin said. "Who here speak English?"

Like metal filings being arranged by a magnet, all heads turned to one young man up front in the middle. He was short, scarcely five feet tall, and skinny. He had a mole at the inside corner of his left eye.

"I speak a little," he said.

"Good," Jiqin said. "You can stay here one week. After that, I charge you ten dollar for one night for one person."

The young man translated for the group, and the smiles slowly faded. Everything now was strictly business. The chatter now was short, clipped.

"*Si, si,*" one man said.

A couple of the women came up and shook Jiqin's hand. "*Gracias*," one young woman said. She had straight black hair down to her butt.

"Gracias."

Only then did they begin to explore the apartment to stake out space to sleep.

Omri was right. We don't see Death in America. In this country, Death is ushered in by men and women wearing white coats in cold white rooms. They adhere to a ritual not unlike the rituals in a church. They bring out their instruments and long faces. They whisper among themselves and with the family. They extract a pecuniary offering. Then, at the appointed time, Death comes in and plucks.

Sometimes, Death plucks *sans* His ministers. But even then, the pluckee is carefully covered in a plastic bag, and delivered to Death's ministers so that they can consecrate the action. They issue papers that certify the plucking. It is rare that the actual plucking is witnessed. In this country, we have seen so few pluckings that we have come to believe that Death is shy. We nurse a distant notion that Death is off on the horizon somewhere coming at some later time. We forget that He is always here.

"*No,*" another man said. Then he rattled something off in Spanish. He was older, but he, too, was short. He was broad in the shoulders and chest with skinny hips and small legs.

The young man with the mole by his eye translated, "He said he was told he could stay here one month at no extra cost."

"One week," Jiqin corrected.

The young man translated.

The older man grew stern. His eyes narrowed, and his gaze darted from side to side. "I have no more money," he said in English.

The others tried to console him in Spanish. One woman tried to put her hand on his shoulder, but he jerked away. He reacted as if her hand were a spider.

"I have no more money," he said again.

Jiqin approached him, but he stepped back sharply. "I have no more money," he said.

Jiqin reached her hand out to him. The man pulled a knife. Someone gasped, "*Juan, no*," as the crowd moved away from Jiqin and Juan standing in the middle of the floor.

Juan looked at the knife as if he had surprised himself. Probably accustomed to pulling his knife at home, he suddenly realized that pulling the knife here was a mistake. Now, not only was he not going to be welcome to stay a month, he knew he was going to have to leave tonight. His changing facial expressions revealed his changing mental state. He furrowed his brow, then relaxed it. He clenched his jaw, then relaxed it. His gaze moved from one spot on the floor to another then to another as if he were searching for money. He was confused. Where was he going to sleep? Where was he going to get money for food? Who, if anyone, would be willing to leave with him? His changing expression told it all. He was alone in a strange country, and he now had no place to go. He was desperate. Maybe he could scare her into letting him stay the night. He lunged at Jiqin with the knife.

Jiqin was swift, and she was accurate. Using the same hand she had used to block my feeble blows that day in the park, she parried the strike up, controlled his wrist, and spun under his arm. Suddenly, she was behind him, and she had the knife. Her thrusts were so quick that I wasn't sure she had really delivered them. Once in the liver, and then straight into the side of his neck. She stepped back in horror, her hands covering her open mouth, as if she were witnessing something someone else had done.

I was so completely fooled by her reaction that I had to look again to see what had been done. That's when Juan dropped to his knees. It looked as if his tiny legs were finally buckling from the weight of his massive upper torso. Then he dropped over onto his face.

There was surprisingly little blood coming from the wound. In all likelihood, his blood was collecting in his lungs and stomach.

The women in the group all looked away. One or two buried their face in a neighbor's shoulder. The men all stared stoically at Juan, all of them except the translator. He puked on himself. Rather he would have puked on himself if he had had anything in his stomach to puke. Instead, he merely heaved. His voice as he heaved was the only sound in the room.

That's when Jiqin surprised me again. I was beginning to think that she was going to do what Ida had done. Cry. Shrink into herself. Fade to nothing. But she didn't. She looked at the translator with a fixed, steely gaze. "Tell them Juan was stupid, and he got what he deserved. Tell them if anyone talk," she said, "they get what Juan got." She drew in a deep breath, then sighed. Then she said, almost matter-of-factly, "I get someone to clean up this mess." She headed for the door, and a path opened in the circle of people. I moved out of the circle, and joined her as she left.

"What are you going to do with the body?" I asked.

"I don't know," she answered.

"Get me a couple of men," I said. "I know what to do."

III

When I was young, I didn't know white people existed except at school or in the news. Where I lived, I didn't even pass them in the street. The first one I ever met went by the name Miss Blue. The irony of a white woman named Miss Blue escaped me at the time, but in later years, I wondered about it. Maybe Mama or Grandma Daughter knew the story behind the name. If they did, they never told me.

What I remembered most about her was that she smelled different. Back in the early fifties, people didn't clean themselves as often as they do today. As a rule, people were pungent. Miss Blue was no exception. I didn't know how old she was, but I thought she was older than Mama and not as old as Grandma Daughter. She was my baby-sitter. Mama would take me to her apartment over on State Street whenever she and Grandma Daughter had someplace special they needed to go.

Miss Blue was a small woman, flat-chested with no curves to her body. She wore straight-cut house dresses in dark blues, greys and browns. She wore black comforts with short heels and shiny, black toe-caps. By her own admission, she did herself up plain. She had small, grey eyes that almost blended in with her pasty face. Her nose was tiny and pinched looking, not full and round like the people I knew. Her lips had permanent creases from where she squeezed them together all the time. By my reckoning, she was an odd duck. Back then, I was too young to understand the message she offered. Now, I understood her perfectly.

Miss Blue was in exile. She was a white woman married to a black man who lived in the black community. Her husband was a cop. His story Mama and Grandma Daughter eventually *did* tell me. According to them, he was one of those black cops that the white police department depended upon to keep order in the Negro neighborhood. And, apparently, he was well-known. Folks knew him as Cop Buck, though his real name was Sydney Beaman. Miss Blue's real name was Faith, Faith Beaman.

According to the stories, Cop Buck was a wild man. He loved it whenever a tavern owner called the police because some patron had consumed too much and had gotten rowdy. He would charge in, night stick swinging. He would thump anybody who was handy. People in the neighborhood hated him.

It was Grandma Daughter who told me that Cop Buck liked to play a game. After whipping people's heads, he would seat himself at a table by a wall, and pull his gun out. He would place the gun on the far side of the table. Then he would dare anybody to go for it. As a rule, no one dared. It was rumored, however, that twice, someone took him up on his dare. Cop Buck fought and killed them both. He liked being in fights to the death.

In all the times I had been at Miss Blue's place, I had never seen Cop Buck. He was always gone. One day, I got my nerve up and asked, "Miss Blue, are you married?" I knew she was, but I couldn't think of any other way to broach the topic of her husband.

Miss Blue liked it when Mama brought me by her house. She always smiled and hugged me. She didn't have children of her own, and in a way, I was kind of a surrogate. And I liked being there. She talked to me the way she would talk to an adult. I was unaccustomed to being talked to that way, and I liked it. Most of the other adults in my life talked down to me. I was a child, and they just didn't have time for me. Miss Blue wasn't like that. Whenever I came by, she would fix warm milk and cookies, and we would sit in the kitchen and talk. Mostly, it was she who talked. But I was a good listener, and I always enjoyed her musings about times past, about riding in buck boards, and raising chickens, and life in Arkansas. I felt as if I knew her in a way that I had never known an adult.

The day I asked if she was married, her face changed. Her little thin smile faded. The creases in her lips became more pronounced. She focused her pale grey eyes off into the corner at the bucket of wood by the big black stove.

Then she folded her bony little hands in her lap. The tendons and veins at the back of her hands pushed hard against the skin. After a few seconds, she looked down at them, and said, "He never liked my dressing."

"Huh?" I asked.

"He never liked my cooking. Said it was too bland. But he especially disliked my dressing. Said it was gooey."

"I like your cooking," I said.

"You've never had my cooking," she said.

"I know, but I like it, anyway."

She smiled, and gave me another cookie. Then the smile faded as she looked over at the bucket of wood again. "I never should have married him," she said. "I never should have married him."

"Why, Miss Blue?"

"You're too young to understand," she said, "but I'm alone. I have no friends. Negroes don't befriend me because I'm white. Whites shun me because I married him. And to top it all off, he's never here. He has girlfriends." She paused, and looked at me. She was probably wondering if she was divulging too much. But she was on a roll. She sighed, and continued, "He comes in, and I can smell the women on him. He doesn't even bother to clean himself up." She paused again. "I have no children. I have no property because my family disowned me. They think I'm a whore. I have nothing. I sit in this house all day, every day waiting for him to come home. And maybe he'll show up, and maybe he won't.

"Oh, but he was something when we were young." Her face became animated at the recollection. "He was big and muscular and black. He wore his head clean-shaven. His features looked as if they had been chiseled in stone, pronounced and angled. His chin, the line of his jaw, his lips, his cheeks, the flare of his nostrils, the ridge over his eyes were all angular. Even his ears had lines that were oddly juxtaposed." Then her face got sad again. "If the folks back home had known what he was doing to me, they would have hanged him. That's why we had to move here."

Miss Blue's sadness infected my whole stay that day. It was the only time that I was glad when Mama came to pick me up.

It wasn't true that she had no friends. She had one. Miss Abbey. Miss Abbey looked just like Miss Blue, except she was bigger than Miss Blue. Bigger and taller. They both wore those straight, formless dresses and plain black shoes with the round toe-caps. But where Miss Blue had thin features, Miss Abbey's features were fleshy, and they drooped. Her eyelids drooped; her jowls drooped; the flesh under her chin drooped. And where Miss Blue was married, Miss Abbey was a spinster.

Miss Abbey came to visit several times when I was there. I wondered why she didn't visit more often, since they seemed to get along so well. Once in a while, Miss Blue would go out shopping, and leave me with Miss Abbey. And Miss Abbey was like Miss Blue in that she talked to me like an adult as well. She never married, because, as she put it, she preferred other women to men. She gave me a curious look when she told me that, as if she was wondering whether or not I understood what she meant. I didn't. And my blank expression must have communicated that fact to her. Because then she got that same far-off look that Miss Blue had gotten, and mused that loneliness was the price to be paid for being too independent.

She was unlike Miss Blue in another way. They didn't smell the same. Miss Abbey had no smell. Sometimes, I preferred Miss Abbey's company to Miss Blue's for that reason.

Miss Abbey confided in me that she had known Miss Blue for many years, since they were young women in Arkansas. She told me that she saved Miss Blue's life once. Miss Blue had diphtheria, and was suffocating on mucous gathered in her throat. Miss Abbey took a thin stick and used it to removed some of the mucous. Miss Blue was able to breathe after that, and soon recovered. She loved Miss Blue, and was heartbroken when Miss Blue ran off to Chicago and married Sydney Beaman. That's when she told me that Miss Blue was the reason that she came to Chicago as well. It was years later that I understood what she meant by that.

IV

It's funny how you don't pick your profession; your profession picks you. Growing up, I had always wanted to be an engineer, someone who built things, cars, houses, bridges. There had always been something intriguing about gathering raw materials and building a tool that could then be used to modify the course of history. I read books about the works of engineers: the New York subway system, the Erie, Suez and Panama Canals, the federal highway system were among the topics I devoured. Later, I wanted to be a poet. But that was just 'cause I wanted to be with Gwen. Both those dreams, however, died in a blaze of glory along with a couple of cops in a secluded near-west side police station. But like the proverbial sphinx, a new reality was born from those ashes. I saw that night for the first time who I really was, a creature. In fact, I had begun calling it . . . me . . . that. The creature. Ida saw it, too, and it scared her. It scared her because she saw the same creature in herself. But it intrigued me. I couldn't rid myself of the thought that I was a dangerous motherfucker. And who knew? Certainly, I didn't. I knew that night that I was capable of anything. *Anything!* All I had to do was think it, and I could do it. But I also knew that I didn't look like who I was. I was the real live wolf in sheep's clothing. That was a part of what made me so dangerous. I was what most people only see in the movies.

I began to look at other people differently. Maybe there were other people like me out there. Not maybe, there *were*. But like they couldn't recognize me, I couldn't recognize them. In a world filled with sheep, there were wolves, wolves that practiced looking like sheep. I became vigilant. I began to look at everyone as if they could be a wolf, a fellow creature. Because, in fact, they could. I began staring men down for sport. On busses, on trains, in elevators, I would stare them straight in the left eye.

The reactions I got were many and varied. Some men looked away as soon as eye contact was made. They looked away scared; they looked away ashamed; they looked away disinterestedly. In my mind, though, it didn't matter. If they looked away, they were sheep. Other men stared back for a second or two, then deliberately looked away. These were the guys that I thought might be most like me, guys who didn't want to blow their cover by appearing too aggressive. Then there were the guys that said, fuck you, and stared back hard. When I met them, *I* looked away so as not to blow *my* cover. I reasoned that those guys were real wolves, but less dangerous than me, because they didn't bother to hide. As a result, they would be easy to locate and pick off.

Jiqin got a couple of her workers to help me. One of them was her uncle. This time, he almost genuflected. Maybe he thought *I* killed Juan. Or maybe he heard Jiqin's warning to the Mexicans, and thought it just might apply to him as well. Maybe he thought I would have him deported. In any case, he was so obsequious, I wanted to smack him and say, stand the fuck up like a man. If ever there were a sheep, he was it.

The other one, the younger of the two, was cool. He wore his hair slicked straight back over his bowling ball-shaped head like Rudolf Valentino. His jet black hooded eyes and the nostrils of his upturned nose looked like the finger holes in the ball. He looked cocky and self-assured like a boxer, like someone who would call himself Kid something or Chico something. Yeah. In my mind, that's who he was. A Chinese Chico. Chico looked at Juan lying dead on the floor, and showed no emotion at all. Then he started looking around for some way to dispose of him.

We wrapped Juan's body in an old carpet that had been stored in the basement for years. Someone had rolled it up and put it down there even before I moved into the place years ago. Really, it was just a remnant. But there was enough to wrap him a couple of times, and tie him with some clothes line. We waited until about three in the morning, then carried him down the back stairs and to the alley. Juan was so short that we hardly had any room to maneuver as the three of us carried him. I was in the front. The sheep was in the middle, and Chico brought up the rear. Nearly stumbling over each other's feet, we carried Juan down the alley to the intersection with the street. We stopped at the edge of the building, and dropped Juan on the concrete. I was being cautious, looking both ways to make sure no one was coming. But Chico didn't hesitate. He stood straight up and walked right out into the middle of the street. Nothing was coming. He pulled a claw hammer from his belt and pried up the steel sewer cover.

I immediately grabbed one end of the rolled up Juan, and began dragging him in the direction of the sewer. The uncle just stood there. I gave him a sustained steely-eyed stare to remind him of who he thought I was, and it worked. He grabbed the other end, the heavy end, and dragged with a vengeance.

Fear is an amazing motivator. With just a little fear, some people perform feats of crystal clarity, incredible speed and enormous strength. Everybody knows this. But not everybody has witnessed it. *I* had never witnessed it. The sheep changed all that. He pulled so hard, I thought he was going to hurt himself. He leaned his entire weight into it. Tendons protruded from his wrists and arms. Blood vessels bulged from his neck. And Juan moved. Slowly at first. But as the sheep strained, Juan gained speed. I pushed a little, but I wanted to see how far the sheep would be able to pull him. He surprised me. He pulled him all the way over to the sewer, then dropped Juan's head over the opening. The sheep then scurried around to where I had been pretending to push, and lifted the end of the roll containing Juan's feet. But Juan's shoulders were too broad. The sheep signaled to Chico with his chin, and Chico knew exactly what to do. He made some exploratory hits along the rolled carpet looking for Juan's collar bones. Then he hit them as hard as he could until they broke. Both of them. I heard them snap. Juan's shoulders slumped in, but still not enough for him to fit into the opening. That's when Chico started working directly on the sides of Juan's shoulders. The bone fragments crunched as he hit them over and over again. Then, all at once, Juan dropped straight in. Actually, he slipped out of the carpet roll and thunked on the sewer floor. The sheep dropped the carpet in for good measure. Then he harrumphed, and snapped his head to one side as a signal to Chico to pull the sewer cover back into place. Chico complied.

Then the sheep did the oddest thing. He looked at me, and winked. The motherfucker winked! Then he led the way back up the alley to the house. Half way there, though, he switched again. He drooped his shoulders, and began to shuffle his feet. For a few minutes at the sewer, he was somebody else. Now, he was the sheep again.

That night in bed, I asked Jiqin about him.

"He is my uncle Master Yuen," she said.

"And?" I asked.

"That's all I can tell you," she said.

"That's all you can tell me? What does *that* mean?"

"That's all I can tell you," she said again. She turned her back to me, curled into the fetal position, and arranged the pillow under her head.

"I thought he was afraid of me," I said.

"Master Yuen is afraid of no one."

"But he always bowed to me."

"Yes," she said.

"But why?

"To show you respect."

I thought about it for a moment. Then I said, "I thought your uncle was a doctor."

"He a doctor," she said. "He heal you. That why we here. That why I in your bed."

"Wait a minute," I said. "Wait just a fucking minute." I sat up in the bed. "You want an arrangement here with me. Well, the way to keep this arrangement is to be honest. If you can't be honest with me, the deal is off."

This time, she thought about it for a moment. Then she sat up in the bed facing me. "Okay," she said. "No more bullshit. You've seen too much for me to continue this charade anyway."

These people were full of surprises. First it was the sheep, or rather Master Yuen. Then it was Jiqin. All of a sudden, the broken English was gone. Was nothing as it appeared?

"My uncle is a doctor, just like I said he was."

"What kind of doctor?" Curiously, the image of an African witch doctor popped into my mind.

"A *medical* doctor," she said. She didn't even bother to try to hide the indignation in her voice. "And he is respected worldwide for the research he has done on exotic viruses."

"So, what's he doing here?"

"He was tricked," she said, "tricked into endorsing the validity of the results of some experiments that were never conducted. He had been shown manufactured data. When he threatened to go to the international press, the government came and arrested him. His supporters bribed the jail personnel, and he was able to escape."

"And from there," I asked, "he came here?"

"Almost," she answered. "It turns out that the escape was a setup. He was supposed to get caught by the warden who would then provide evidence at Uncle's trial of the attempted escape."

"So what happened?"

"Uncle escaped anyway. In the process, the warden was killed."

"Did your uncle kill him?"

"That part isn't clear. Uncle says no, but they did fight. And the warden was no match for uncle."

"Meaning?"

"Uncle studied with the Shaolin monks."

"So what about you and that phoney accent?"

"I use the accent to avoid having to talk too much," she said. "If people think you don't understand them, they are less likely to want to be around."

"Are you running from the law, too?"

"No," she answered. "The law is satisfied that I am here legally."

"Well, are you?"

"Not exactly."

"Should I take that as a no?"

"I have a green card."

"Then you're here legally."

"It's a fake."

"So get a real one."

"I don't have a sponsor."

"I'll sponsor you."

"It's not that easy."

"How so?"

"We would need to be married, and you would need to be more than Jay Sam Guy."

That stopped me cold. Here I was pressuring her into being open and honest, and my entire existence was a lie. More than that, Jiqin knew it was a lie. As much as anything, I was surprised that she was that astute. "Right," I said, "we are not getting married."

I had thought I was ending the conversation, but I guess she was on a roll. "Fine," she said, "we don't have to be married. But what about the honesty part?"

I knew what she was asking. I just wasn't ready to answer. "What about it?" I asked back.

"Are we going to do a show and tell, or not?"

"I don't know."

"You brought it up," she said. "I'm perfectly content to not know. Apparently, you are not."

"I wanted to know about your uncle."

"And I told you," she said. "Now I want to know about you."

"What's to know?" I was playing coy.

"*You* tell *me*."

I thought about it for a moment. My story was too long and unbelievable. Then it hit me. I looked her straight in the eye, and said, "I *am* the Buddha."

"I know that part," she said. "Tell me something I *don't* know."

Damn this bitch! Who did she think she was, pressing me to the wall like this.

"For example," she continued, "why have you become Jay Sam Guy? That's not who you were born. What's up with that?"

I thought about it a moment, then decided to tell her the whole story. I told her about Uncle Buddy, Mighty Red, Lillie. I told her about the shooting at Rainbow Park, and how it now meant that I was free, that I no longer had to sneak around, that since my enemies now thought I was dead, I could start a new life. I could do and be anything I wanted.

When I finished, she looked at me. Her expression wasn't one of awe or admiration. Neither was it one of loathing or disgust. I don't know what it was, but it wasn't her normal expression. "Well," I said, "you wanted to know. Happy?"

She smiled. Again, it wasn't her normal smile. "You'll need papers," she said. "I can get them for you."

"The same folks who made your green card?"

"When do you want to have been born?" she asked.

V

I was surprised at how easy it was slipping into my new life. Jiqin had been right. Papers were as easy to get as bubble gum at a sweet shop. I took the name Jason Samuel Guy, and picked December 25th of my actual birth year as my new birth date. I figured that would be easy to remember. And our life together seemed easier now. There was an openness between us that made her real comfortable to be with. Jiqin was becoming more of a wife than either of my real wives had ever been. Even her uncle seemed to be taking to me. He wanted to teach me kung fu, but I told him no. I told him Jiqin would protect me. He didn't like that very much, but he didn't push.

"Maybe later," he said.

"Yeah," I said, "maybe later."

All the Mexicans were gone after about two weeks. And we had money. Human trafficking was a lucrative line of work. The Chinese workers that were her crew still lived downstairs. We rarely saw them, though. They lived their lives, and we lived ours. Until there was a job to be done, of course. Life was good.

Maybe it was too good. There's a law of balance in the universe. If shit gets too good, something comes along and fucks it up. Sometimes, that something will be obvious, like getting hit by a car right after hitting the lottery. But other times, it's obscure. The fuck up that came this time was one of the obscure kinds. In fact, it was so obscure, I didn't even recognize it as a fuck up.

We were sitting on a bench by Thorndale Beach on the north side, Jiqin and I. It was a Sunday. We sat along the lake shore looking out over the sand and the water. Seagulls squawked overhead. Children splashed in the waves rolling in. A soft wind blew, and I could feel myself wanting to doze in the sun. In the distance, I could hear the tinkling of bells as an ice cream vendor pushed his cart along the path. It was pleasant enough. In fact, I began to imagine licking ice cream and feeling the melted confection sticky on my hand as I pulled the paper down for a clear bite. I was about to ask Jiqin if she wanted something when a cop car squawked breaking my revery. It sounded like a giant seagull. I turned my head to see. Sure enough a blue-and-white cruised over the lawn crushing the grass beneath its mud-encrusted tires. I looked back along the path it formed in the grass, and the tire tracks clipped the corner of one of the flower beds between us and the street. One of the flowers, a yellow one, was completely crushed into the dirt. The wind rolled one of the loose petals into the space between the tire tracks.

The cop in the shotgun seat rolled his window down. "Hey, you," he shouted to the vendor. "Get over here!"

The vendor, a short Mexican with a stomach that sagged over his belt, pushed his cart towards the police prowler. He reminded me of Juan, and I wondered whether or not Juan's body had ever been found. I figured that a body having been found in a sewer wasn't the kind of thing that would make the evening news.

Because of the wind rustling the leaves of a nearby Cottonwood tree, I could not hear what was being said. But from his body movements, I could tell that he was asking them what kind of ice cream they wanted. The driver opened his door and exited the car. He was big, a full foot taller than the vendor. The bulletproof vest he wore made him look even bigger. The corners of his vest pushed against his blue shirt giving his upper body a mechanical, almost robotic appearance. He looked like a machine as he squared the corner en route around the front of the car. He flipped open the cart cover, and began pushing the contents from one side to the other looking for what he wanted. He looked like a bear clawing through a beehive for honey. The vendor protested by his gestures. Just then, the wind died down.

"You better shut the fuck up," the cop said, "or I'll haul your ass to the station and take *all* your ice cream."

He flipped a cone to his partner, grabbed one for himself, then got back into the car and drove off. He gassed the car so hard, it fish-tailed in the grass leaving two 'S'-shaped streaks where the grass had been plowed away by the tires.

The vendor stood for a moment dumfounded. Looking at him, I almost felt guilty that Juan had to be killed. Then he closed the lid on his cart and pushed it back toward the path. After a few seconds, he began tinkling the bells.

"Let's go," I said to Jiqin.

"What's the matter," she said.

"We need to expand our operation," I answered.

"Oh," she said. "Into what? Drugs? We don't do drugs."

"Not drugs," I answered. "Assassinations. We need to kill somebody."

Master Yuen allowed himself one small smile when I told him I was ready to study kung fu. "I teach you good," he said. "You protect Jiqin."

Fool that I was, I thought studying kung fu would be fun and easy. After all, whenever Master Yuen gave a demonstration, it looked fun and easy. It was smooth and fluid looking. But he changed my mind on the very first day.

He got up early, and the first thing he did was put on a kettle for tea. More than a kettle, really. He put a two-gallon pot of water on to boil, then he dropped in a couple of handfuls of loose green tea. I wondered as I watched him stir it who the hell all this tea was going to be for. I learned the hard way. It was for me.

After he put on the tea, we talked. He assured me that he wasn't going to teach me the way he had been taught in China. That way was too hard, he said. He was going to teach me the easy way. Then he showed me some warmup stretches. He started with head rolls to stretch the muscles in the neck. Next came shoulder rolls and pulls, wrist rolls and pulls, finger bends, trunk twists and bends, back leans, hip rolls in both directions, knee rolls in both directions, deep knee bends, ankle rolls and toe flexes and bends.

Next we did leg stretches. With my back against a wall, he lifted my leg as high as he could get it. My Achilles tendon was resting on his shoulder as he locked my knee down with his hands to pull the hamstring. I was feeling proud to be able to get my leg that high until he said, "Don't worry. I've seen worse." Then he stretched my legs to the side to pull the tendons at the groin. Finally, he had me do splits, American and Chinese. I was already exhausted. He said, "Good. Now we can get started."

I looked over at the clock. We had been at this for about forty minutes. Master Yuen walked over to the clock and turned its face to the wall. He used a ladle to issue some tea into a glass.

"Drink," he said, "You'll feel better."

He had me do sit-ups, crunches, leg lifts and jumping jacks by the score. I did about sixty of each.

"Wow," I said, feeling proud of myself. "Sixty is a lot."

He smiled and nodded his head slightly. "Two thousand is lot."

I was stunned. As I stood wondering whether or not a person could even do two thousand crunches, he started me on push-ups. I did twenty. I was afraid to express any kind of pride. I looked over at

Master Yuen. I could tell that he knew what I was thinking, but he said nothing. Just as well. I couldn't even imagine two thousand push-ups.

We worked on punches, kicks, blocks, locks, holds, escapes, balance and strategies. We did that all day, every day for months. After a while, he introduced me to weapons, knives, swords, sticks, bows and arrows, darts, pistols, rifles, and explosives. We covered it all. He introduced me to things that could be used as weapons: belts, string, cards. He taught me cover, stealth, and camouflage. Then one day, he surprised me.

"You no longer need me," he said.

"What?!" I was confused.

"You're ready," he said.

"But . . ., but . . .," I said. "I don't *feel* ready."

"If you feel ready, you're not," he said. "When you need it, it will be there." He emptied the pot of tea, then turned and walked into his room, and closed the door.

In a flash, I remembered all those martial arts movies with the bad dubbing I had seen as a kid. The master leaves or is killed, and the student always feels abandoned. Now I knew why. I felt like a child in the wilderness, uncertain of his ability to survive. In the end, though, I had to trust his judgment. It didn't matter how I felt. My training was over, and I had to move on.

Looking for my first hit, I felt like Robin Hood, a protector of the weak. But I wasn't after money. I was after justice. I remembered the job Ida and I had pulled years ago. It virtually killed her, but it made me feel alive. The rush of adrenaline, the danger. I loved it!

I scanned the news papers for stories of police misconduct. I looked at big stories from New York to California. I thought about Mark Fuhrman, but decided that the publicity around the O.J. trial made him too risky. Besides, O.J. got off. Then I found a small story in a small neighborhood newspaper in Chicago about the death of Marcus Pemberly at the hands of one of the Chicago Police Department's finest. This was it. Showtime.

It was luck, really. I had no idea how I was going to find the guy, so I started by listening to the account of the incident on television. They never give the address of an incident on the local news, but they always give the neighborhood. The neighborhood was the north side not far from the lake. I stopped at a tavern over on Broadway near Lawrence. I bellied up to the bar and ordered a beer. I deliberately sat near a brother who was in a heated conversation with the barmaid.

He was a tall man with long legs, so he had to sit on the barstool with his knees wide apart in order to be able to get close enough to be right in her face as he talked.

"You a fool if you believe that," he said, "a motherfuckin' fool."

"Why?" She defended herself, "Just because I don't believe what you believe?"

The man sat back exasperated. Then he turned to me, "Would you tell this bitch that oranges got more vitamin C than any other fruit on the planet."

"I don't know that, brother," I said. "I don't know how much vitamin C other fruits have."

"That's my point," he said. "If some other fruit had more vitamin C, we would've heard about it."

"I don't listen to the news much," I said, "so I wouldn't know."

"Well, I listens to the news all the motherfuckin' time," he said, "and I ain't heard shit."

The barmaid was a big woman with relatively small tits. Her tits looked like pecs on a male body builder. She had fat cheeks with dimples and big lips that turned down at the corners when she smiled.

"Sorry, boo," she said, "hip-hop news ain't news."

The brother was visibly irritated. He clenched his teeth as he looked back and forth between the barmaid and me.

"What did you hear about the young brother up this way not long ago who hanged himself in his cell?" As much as anything, I asked the question to get the brother's mind off the vitamin issue.

"Hanged hisself!" he said. "When?"

"I heard about it," the barmaid answered.

"You did?" the brother asked. "When? What happened?"

"The boy got busted sticking up a beauty shop," she said.

"A beauty shop?!"

"And when the cops got there, he pulled a gun."

"Wha-a-t?"

"And it was a big gun, too. Or so they said. The cops didn't waste no time dragging his ass off to the slammer."

"Where did it happen?" I asked. "Do you know?"

She hesitated a moment.

"What's the matter?" I asked.

"I'm wondering how much I should tell you," she said.

"What does *that* mean?"

She hesitated again, then said, "I knew the boy. His mama and me went to school together."

My heart leaped. I wanted to blurt out question after question after question. Where did he live? What was his mother's name? Who were the witnesses? But I didn't want to come off as overly eager. I looked away shyly, and said, "Oh." I let the silence between us hang there. I wanted her to volunteer the information. She inhaled sharply.

That's when the brother piped up. "Well, goddamn it, say

something. Tell us what happened."

She exhaled slowly as she cut her gaze to him. "You are such a clown, Jake. I ain't telling you shit."

I wanted to do more than cut him with a gaze. My heart was pounding in my chest. I wanted to punch him in the mouth. I lifted my glass slowly, and took a long swig.

"Aw, c'mon, baby." Jake's voice was smooth. He reached for her hand and pulled it to his lips. "You know I love you." He placed a soft kiss just behind her knuckles. As he did, he caressed her palm with the tip of his index finger.

She recoiled in mock indignation. "You so crazy," she said. "I don't care how much you love me, I ain't telling you shit." She stuck her hand right under his nose. "Kiss my hand again." Then she yanked it away before he could respond. "Ne-ver mind." She turned her attention slowly in my direction. "Marcus Pemberly was Bebe's son. Bebe and me used to run together back in the day. I hadn't talked to her in some years, really. But when I read that story in the paper about somebody with that name dying in the police station, I called her. I mean, how many people do you know named Marcus Pemberly? None, right? So I called her. I hadn't seen Marcus since he was five years old. He was a cute little boy, and proud as he could be. I called him Marc once. And you know that boy corrected me. He folded his little arms and said his name was Marcus, not Marc. 'Call me Marcus,' he said. And I did. Marcus Pemberly."

She turned to the sink and picked up a rag and wet it and began wiping down the bar.

"So I says to Bebe how sorry I am, right? And she breaks down crying. I mean I could hear it in her voice that she had been crying all along, but hearing my voice after all them years and her son having just been killed, it was too much. She broke down sobbing. And then, damn, I broke the fuck down, too. So for a solid minute, there we are, two grown ass women crying on the phone. Not talking, just crying. It was sick, you know? It was sick, but it was cool. And after a minute, we sniffed, and she started talking."

By now, she was done with the bar, and was arranging glasses on her side of the bar. They clinked together as she moved them around.

"In truth, he hadn't done anything. There was no beauty shop robbery, no gun, no nothing. They made all that up for the press, and put the word out to the beauty shop owner that she better back up the story. They picked him up because he looked like somebody they were supposed to have been looking for. They said he was robbing the store so they would have probable cause to lock him up. Bebe went down to the station over on Clark Street, but they wouldn't let her see him. She sat there for four hours before they came out and said he was dead."

The glasses were all in place. So now she re-arranged the ice with the ice scoop. Each thrust of the scoop made that crushed-ice sound.

"Bebe even told me the cop's name. Avel something or other. I just remember the Avel part."

The ice was done, and so was her story. I stood up to leave. She looked over at Jake.

"You gon' buy me something to eat?" she asked.

"We got food at home," he said.

"I don't want nothing we got in that house."

As I pushed the exit door open, I could hear her saying to Jake, "I want you to buy me some shrimp for when I get off."

I stepped out into the daylight. I had a name, but I needed more. I needed a way to get information about the name. I needed to know who Avel was. I wondered if Reverend Milton could help me.

VI

"Beware of anyone who claims on any issue to have the mind of the Lord."

"I know," I answered. "I don't trust anyone who walks around with a Bible in his hand, except you."

"Well, don't even trust me if I claim to know the mind of the Lord. To begin with, the Lord ain't got no mind. The mind is a function of the brain, and God ain't got no brain 'cause God ain't got no body."

We were standing outside the Salvation Army building up on Broadway. We called it Sally's. I used to stand out there a couple of times a week when I was moving around incognito. It was a known place to pick up moving jobs that paid cash with no questions asked. It was also on the other side of town from where I lived. This was in Uptown. I lived in South Shore.

"And the corollary," Milton continued, "is that language does not apply to God. God is beyond the scope of language, and beyond the grasp of the mind. In the sense that the mind can know, God cannot be known."

"What is that supposed to mean?"

"You ain't no dummy," he said, "you know what it means."

"Well, humor me. Pretend that I don't know. It sounds like you're saying God cannot be known."

"That's not what I said. What I said was, God cannot be known with the mind."

"But that's how we know things, with the mind."

"No, it isn't," he corrected. "We know things with the gut."

"We digest food with the gut," I said. "We think and know with the brain."

"You've got a long way to go," he said, shaking his head slowly from side to side.

Reverend Milton was a huge man, six foot six, two hundred and fifty pounds. His hairline formed an "M" over his high and broad forehead. We used to work together whenever we could. He was old enough to be my father, and he took to the job eagerly after he learned that my real father died when I was very young. "Every boy needs a father," he told me, "even if the boy is over 21." Even his voice was big and booming. He sounded like he should have been a movie star. But quite frankly, I wasn't looking for a father or even a father figure. I reckoned that I didn't need one. I had, after all, reached majority without his or anyone else's help, thank you very much. But the day he said that boys needed fathers, I heard it as old men need young men to look up to them. And for whatever reason, I thought having him around might enhance my cover, so I acquiesced.

"You think you know everything," he had told me, "but you don't. You ain't lived long enough to know everything."

"And you have?" I had asked him.

"No, but I been around a whole hell of a lot longer than you, and I know stuff that you don't even know need to be known."

I didn't get a chance to retort, because a guy in an old, faded sand-colored Peugeot station wagon pulled up looking for some men to help him move. The guy was a skinny brother with a short 'fro and a full beard. He had bulbous eyes like Peter Lorre, and crooked yellow teeth.

"I need a few good men," the brother said.

"Me and this boy right here is all the Marines you need," Milton said latching onto my elbow. "Let's go."

He pushed me into the back seat. He rode shotgun. We couldn't have driven more than a block from Sally's before Milton started in again. "Young blood here is my play son," he said to the brother. "I'm teaching him the ins and outs of life."

"Good for you," the brother said. His voice sounded small following Milton's.

We worked all day moving that brother. At the end, he gave us some good money. Apparently, he liked the service we provided. On the walk back to the train station, Milton surprised me. "A man on the lam got to be careful who he work for. Maybe even need somebody to run interference for him."

I hadn't told him I was on the lam. I hadn't told anyone. So I wasn't sure how or even whether he knew what he was talking about. "I'm not sure what you mean," I said, feeling him out.

"Cut the bullshit, son," he said. "I see what I see, and I know what I know. You got to be careful who you work for and work with."

I never questioned him again after that. He negotiated all the deals with the people who stopped by looking for folks to help them move. He also did most of the work. But we split the money 50-50. That was his arrangement.

In time, I did begin to look up to him, and the advice he gave me was always sage. That's why, years later, I was trying to seek his advice again. "People's image of God is limited by their imaginations," Milton was warming to his topic. "People can't imagine God without a body even though they say He's only spirit."

"So, can you help me?" I cut in.

"You still running?" he asked.

"Yeah," I answered, "but not as fast. That's not what I need help with."

I waited for him to ask me what I wanted. He didn't, so I continued, "I need information on a cop named Avel something or other."

"What do you need to know?"

"Everything."

"*Why* do you need to know it?"

"It's part of a project I'm working on," I answered.

"What kind of project?"

"He hurt somebody."

"I know that," he said. "What I want to know is what that has to do with you."

I hesitated for a moment too long.

"Look, son," he said, "I ain't never asked you why you running or who you running from. But I'm gon' give you some free advice. Leave Officer Avel alone."

"He's a murderer," I protested.

"They all murderers, son. That was the one credential they needed to get the job. In order to get the job, they had to have killed somebody in somebody's war somewhere. That's the one thing that qualified them to be cops in the first place. But you can't fix all the wrongs that all the cops in this city have done."

"I can try," I answered. "I can try."

"You'll be sorry," he said.

Then he started telling me about the Marcus Pemberly case. I couldn't help but wonder, though, how he knew what he knew. The information he gave me was simply too detailed for it to have come from folks in the street. I was an ex-street person. I knew the kind of stuff street people knew. This wasn't it. And just like he had never asked me anything about my past, I had never asked him anything about his. Until now, that is.

"I *am* a cop," he answered after I clumsily posed the question. "Or rather, I used to be. I still know some folks in the department."

The expression on my face must have betrayed my surprise. He rocked his head back and laughed with that huge voice.

Then he said, "When we first met right here in front of this very building, I had recently finished doing twenty years in a federal prison."

My expression must have betrayed me again, because he laughed again, though not quite as loudly.

"I was a good cop," he said, "maybe the only one on the force. I went after bad guys for real. Especially drug dealers. What I didn't know was that these dealers were on the FBI's payroll. So they set me up. The FBI busted me for trying to bust them. While I was still on the inside, I got word that one of the main guys I was after laid the ground work that led to the raid on the Black Legion office."

It had been years since I had given much thought to that raid. It was odd that Milton would be the one to remind me of it, and to have indirectly had a connection to it. I remembered Felton Kirby and his boney little wife, Lois. I remembered Felton Junior. All of them died that night in that raid. I remembered the account of Felton, a big man with nappy, rust-colored hair, charging into the police, and beating one of them to death with a club. It was that raid that led to my first blow for freedom. Being reminded of it was a good sign. I remembered the brother I had seen standing across the street from the Legion office taking pictures. Ida had identified him as an FBI agent. I wondered if he was the same guy Milton had been trying to arrest for drug trafficking.

"But who's giving the orders?" I asked. "Ordinary agents and cops aren't the ones out here mandating that drugs be distributed to the community. They might be a part of the trafficking on a lower level, like your guy. But these plans seem to be getting passed along from generation to generation at the upper levels of government. Who are these people who are always in power and always formulating these twisted plans to poison us? They must be part of a think tank or secret society or something. They're like seagulls, and we are the fish. As fish, we can't even see them. We don't even know they're there. So we can't protect ourselves from them. But they *are* there. And our inability to see them is part of their plan. They don't want us to know that we're being exterminated. As seagulls, they literally swoop out of the blue, dive into the water, and snatch us to an instant death."

Reverend Milton's big shoulders sagged. "I can't answer that one," he said. "I spent twenty years asking that same question. Eventually, I gave up. I started reading the Bible instead."

"The answer ain't in the Bible," I said.

"I know, but reading it helped ease the pain of not having the answer to that question."

The Reverend looked ashamed of having been broken, of not having the answer to the biggest question ever: Who's *really* running the show in America?

"But this is what I figured out," he said after a long pause. "The plan is masterful. The formulators of the plan put rules into place for the common man to follow, because as long as he is busy following the rules, he won't even conceive of the notion that there is a plan in place, a plan that he ain't part of. The United States Constitution was put into place to give the people the illusion that they are masters of their own destiny. An elaborate system of government was created with seeming checks and balances, with seeming recourse for injustices, with seeming rules for the way the country is run. But it's a fake. It's all a fake. Oh, it works on a certain low level. And the working on that level helps perpetuate the fiction that it works on all levels. It helps perpetuate the fiction that there is no master plan in place. That's part of the beauty of the plan. As people see the every day workings of government, they begin to believe what they see. After a while, when evidence of how things really work surfaces– briberies, stolen elections, political favors, cronyism, assassinations– the people see *them* as abnormalities, aberrations. It's like a magician setting up an act. He shows you a canary in a cage. When he shows you an empty cage, you think there's something wrong. So he shows you a different canary, and you're satisfied. In truth, the cage is always supposed to be empty. We expect a canary, because we are conditioned to expect a canary. There's never any applause when the canary re-appears, because the people never know that they've been duped. Their only reward is blissful ignorance. Their only reward is that of the fool."

"So going after Avel is worthless," I mused aloud.

"Give unto Caesar that which is Caesar's."

"*Nothing* is Caesar's," I answered. "Caesar gets only what I decide to give him."

"Forget about Officer Avel," he said. "He's just a footnote in the plan. In fact, the formulators *want* you to go after Avel. That's the proof they need that the plan is still working."

"But if not him," I mused aloud again, "who?"

"Indeed," Milton said. "Who, indeed?"

He hesitated a moment, then reached into his pocket and slipped me a crumpled up piece of brown paper bag. I unfolded it. There was a phone number, an address and a name scrawled in pencil and scarcely visible against the wrinkles and folds of the paper. The graphite itself was smeared. The writing was barely legible, but I made it out. The name was Tina Pemberly.

VII

"Who is Tina Pemberly?" I asked.

"That's Marcus Pemberly's mother," Milton answered.

"How did you . . . ," I was going to ask how he knew this was the person I was looking for, but he cut me off.

"I didn't," he said. "I got this information for my own use."

"I'm confused," I said.

"I know you are." He hesitated. Then he looked me straight in the eye, and said, "Maybe it's time I came clean. I know who you are, and I know what you did."

I answered with as much resolve as I could muster. I said, "Huh?"

"I said I know . . ."

I cut him off. "I know what you said," I said. "I don't know what you meant."

"You know what I meant," he said. "You're just not sure you can acknowledge it, because you didn't know anyone else knew."

He was right on both counts. I knew he was alluding to the blow Ida and I had struck for freedom years ago. I also did *not* know that anyone besides Ida and me knew about it. I was cautious with my question.

"How do you know?" I asked.

"I worked out of the station you hit," he answered. "One of the guys you gunned down helped the FBI set me up."

"What makes you think it was me?"

"Ida," he replied.

His answer stunned me. I hadn't known anyone knew who or where Ida even was.

That night years ago destroyed her. She killed a man, saw the creature in me, and, more importantly, she saw the creature in herself. Maybe that's why she lost the baby. It was more than she could handle. After her D & C at Cook County Hospital, the doctor recommended that she get counseling, because she seemed to be more depressed than was normal for having had a miscarriage. He arranged for her to see a staff psychiatrist. Within a year, she was being treated in Kankakee. I visited her a few times, if for no other reason than to assure myself that she wasn't spilling the beans about what happened that night. She didn't even know who I was. She literally sat on the floor cradling an imaginary baby to her bosom. Or maybe it wasn't a baby at all. Maybe it was the ghost of a cop.

"How did you find her?" I asked.

"The doctor who was treating her ratted her out. My partner went out on the follow-up."

"Your partner?" Now there were *two* other people who knew.

"I was in prison, remember? The doctor told Bruce-- that's my partner-- what Ida had said, and Bruce wrote up a report."

"And?"

"And nothing," he said. "She was a crazy woman. Nobody believed her story. Nobody except me and Bruce."

"Why did *you* believe it?"

"I believed it because Bruce believed it. He believed it because she knew details that only the cops and the killers knew."

"Such as?"

"Such as the make and model of the weapons used."

"So how did you link it to me?" I asked.

"Based on Ida's tip, Bruce tracked down the pictures that were taken of the Black Legion office by the punk I had been trying to bust. On the day these pictures were taken, only two people were in the office,

Ida and some man."

"And you think that man was me."

"I'm coming to that part," he said. "Bruce blew the picture of the man up, and showed it to her. She didn't say yes or no. But her reaction changed enough that Bruce was sure who it was."

"So then?"

"So then nothing. We had no idea where to even start looking, and Ida gave us no clue. But after I got out of prison, I started looking for work at Sally's. Then one day, you showed up. I knew instantly who you were."

"Why didn't you turn me in?"

"Turn you in?! You avenged me. Why would I turn you in? All I wanted was to shake your hand."

"That's why you took me under your wing."

"Bingo," he said. "Now, you're beginning to understand."

An eerie feeling came over me. For years, I had assumed that Ida and I had committed the perfect crime. Now, years later, I learn that not just one, but two other people knew about it. I felt vulnerable. I resisted the impulse to look over my shoulder.

"So, now what?" I asked. "Why are you telling me this?"

"I got Tina Pemberly's information because I wanted to help."

"Help how?" I asked. "She's going to think you are what you are, a bum."

"Yes," he said, "that's the reason I haven't done anything with the information until now."

"What's changed? She's still going to think you're a bum."

"That's where you come in."

"Where I come in? I've got my own plan for this project."

"I know," he said, "but maybe we can help each other."

For the first time since I'd known him, I was having trouble trusting Milton. Ignorance truly is bliss. As long as I thought my secret was mine alone, everything was fine. But now that I knew that Milton-- and Bruce, too, for that matter-- knew my secret, everything was different.

"I don't know," I said. "I'm not sure I want to work with another partner. I let Ida be my partner the last time, and look what it got me."

"You can't do it alone," he said.

"I know how to do a hit," I said, acknowledging for the first time my involvement in the caper years ago.

"That part's easy," he said. "How much advance research did you do for that job?"

"Almost none. We just picked a target, and hit it. It was like a target of opportunity."

"Exactly," he said. Then he asked, "How much research are you doing this time?"

His point was made. There were already people whom I have had to question in order to get as far as I had gotten. Now I was facing the prospect of talking to Tina Pemberly.

"What did you have in mind?" I asked.

"We'll do the leg work; you do the hit."

"We?"

"Me and Bruce."

Damn! In the span of thirty seconds, I had gone from no partners to two partners. That eerie feeling was growing.

"I've got to think about this," I said.

"What's to think about?"

I didn't want to have to confess to the eerie feeling, so I played the need-for-time card.

"I'm not good at making snap decisions," I said. "I just need to sleep on it."

That night, Jiqin gave all the signals. She rubbed my foot with hers; she mock yawned; she nudged me with her behind. I ignored them all. She took her panties off and rubbed them in my face.

"What?" I said.

"What do you mean 'what?' I want you to screw me."

"Not tonight," I said. I turned over and pulled the cover over my shoulder.

"What?" she said.

"What do you mean 'what?' I'm not in the mood."

"Not in the mood?"

"What?!" I said again.

"What do you mean you're not in the mood?"

"I mean I don't want to screw you, because I'm preoccupied."

"Wait a minute," she said. She sat up. "When *you* want to screw and *I'm* not in the mood, we screw. But when *I* want to screw and *you're* not in the mood, we don't screw. What's wrong with this picture?"

She had a point. It's like we were married. Humph. Who was I kidding? There was no like about it. We *were* married. We were more married than any of my other wives and I had ever been.

"I've got a problem," I said.

"Maybe I can help," she said. Her interest was genuine.

"There's a part of the story that I haven't told you," I said. "A part that at the time didn't matter."

"Now it does?" she asked.

"Now it does."

I was resigned to the fact that someone else was going to have to know what Ida and I had done. I took solace in the notion of picking that someone.

I told her everything. I told her that Ida and I had committed murder. I told her that we attacked and killed police officers at a small and remote police station in retaliation for an attack the police had launched on the Black Legion office. The Black Legion, I explained, was an organization dedicated to the cause of freeing Black people in the United States of America. I hadn't been a member, but Ida had. She had joined at the urging of two of our close friends, Felton and Lois Kirby, who were also members.

The office had been under surveillance for weeks by an operative of the FBI. Then one night, they struck. A meeting was being held that night, and members were there with their families. Under the guise of breaking up a dope selling ring, the police broke in. Claiming that Legion members resisted arrest, they killed almost everyone there. Felton, Lois and their son, Felton Junior, were killed in that raid.

Shortly thereafter, Ida and I decided to conduct a counter raid. We bought a couple of rifles, and I showed her how to use them. We picked a target, and we struck.

We were really lucky. We did virtually no planning. We picked a small police station on the near west side, and simply walked in. I shot the desk sergeant, and Ida shot another officer who emerged from a nearby office. She shot him in the face. Granted, it was late at night, but nobody else came out to challenge us. We threw Molotov cocktails into the corners, and left.

Ida had been pregnant at the time. However, the stress of killing a man caused her to lose the baby. Eventually, it drove her mad. Not everyone is cut out to be a killer. I told Jiqin that I had thought we had committed the perfect crime. I told her about my living as a street person for years until that day she rescued me in the park. I even told her where Ida was now out in Kankakee.

Then I told her about Milton and Bruce. I told her the arrangement Milton had offered.

"So, what's the problem?" she asked.

"The problem is that I don't know if I want more partners." I said, "I have a partner. You."

I didn't mean for it to sound like I was in love with her, but apparently, it did. Her face got that soft, weepy look that women in love get. By now, I was sitting up, too. So she crawled over into my lap, and sort of melted with her arms around my neck. Hell. Maybe I did mean it.

"I love you," she said.

I wasn't going to reply, but the words came up like a belch. "I love you, too," I said.

After that, how could we *not* screw?

VIII

I rolled off of Jiqin exhausted. She was the best she had ever been. I came deep inside of her. Twice. She than crawled on top of me and lay with her head on my chest breathing heavily. We must have lain like that for twenty minutes.

"Does Milton know about us?" she asked finally.

I knew she was referring to her crew and uncle.

"Certainly not," I answered.

"Then let him help you. If he gets to be a problem, we're here to back you up."

I waited a while before deciding to thank her. But by the time I got around to forming the words, she twitched. I knew she was asleep.

That night, I had the oddest dream. They always say that if you fall in a dream and don't wake up, you're dead. The reason is that the natural reflex of the body to tighten up to brace for the fall will wake you. I don't know who figured that one out, because only someone who had died would know if it was true. Then there is the obvious problem of communicating what was learned back to those still living. Still, that's what they say.

In this dream, I was riding my bicycle in Grant Park by the lake across from Buckingham Fountain. Suddenly, a fog rolled in that was so dense, I couldn't see anything around me. I couldn't see the ground; I couldn't see my hands on the handlebars. But I could still feel the wind on my face, and the pedals under my feet still offered resistance. I could hear a voice somewhere near me pleading, *"No mas! No Mas!"* The voice was tiny like Jiqin's, but I knew it was Juan begging for his life. I couldn't see where I was going, but, somehow, I knew where to steer. It was as if I had the road memorized. The turns I was making did not correspond to the actual bends in the path along the lake in Grant Park. I didn't know where I was.

Then, without warning, I hit a pothole in the path. The bike stopped cold. I didn't. I sailed over the handlebars, and headed straight for the ground that I still couldn't see. This is where I guess I thought I should have flinched. I hit the ground, and the ground was soft. Well, not soft. Just not hard, either. The overall sensation was comfortable. Hitting the ground was comfortable, and the incongruity woke me up. I didn't have to open my eyes. I could feel that I was cuddled behind Jiqin. I could smell her hair and skin. I could smell her pussy. I was overcome with a feeling of well-being so powerful that it bordered on bliss. I was supposed to be the protector, but holding Jiqin like that made me feel like the one being protected. I felt safe. I drew in a deep breath, and slipped back into slumber.

The following morning was Sunday. Her boys didn't have any place to go, so the house seemed alive with activity. Somebody was running a vacuum cleaner. Somebody else was hammering something into the wall. And I couldn't be sure, but it sounded like someone was running water full blast in the bathroom.

Jiqin stirred next to me.

"What's going on?" I asked.

She yawned. "Another shipment is coming in tonight." She got up and headed for the toilet.

"Mexicans?" I asked.

She didn't close the door, so I could hear her in there taking a piss. "Yes," she answered. "They came across the border yesterday."

"How much will you get this time?"

"We'll get the same amount," she said, "five hundred dollars each."

I sat for a moment pondering where the money from the last

shipment had gone, and wondering what the dollar amount of this shipment would be.

Then, as if she had been reading my mind, she said, "We have a lot of people here to feed. It takes money. Lots of it." She paused for a long moment, then asked, "How much can you get for assassinations?"

"I don't know," I answered. "Depends on the client."

She thought about it for a minute, then mused, "I wonder how much the government pays."

"They have their own assassins. Besides, they're not going to let someone wanted by the INS do killings for them."

"Maybe, maybe not," she said.

"Besides," I said, "I know who I'm after."

"Who?" she asked.

"Dirty cops," I said.

She yawned. "Dirty cops? There's no money in killing them."

My choice of targets obviously fell flat with Jiqin.

I got up and took a shower and got dressed. By the time I got downstairs, the kitchen was crowded with folks foraging for food. Master Yuen was at the stove fixing sticky rice. Jiqin was whisking eggs in a bowl. Chico stood in a corner with one foot on a chair eating a banana. The whole scene was one of controlled chaos.

I usually fixed toast and jam and tea for myself for breakfast. In fact, we all usually fixed whatever it was that we wanted for ourselves. So when Jiqin said, "Sit down; I'm fixing these for you," everybody stopped what they were doing. Master Yuen looked over at Chico and winked. Chico affected a love-struck grin, and fluttered his eyes.

"Ignore these assholes," Jiqin said. "I can fix you eggs if I want to."

She sautéed them in butter, and served them to me with a serving of Master Yuen's sticky rice. Then she kissed me on the forehead, and left the room. I guessed that she was going to take a shower or something.

As soon as she was gone, Master Yuen sat in the chair across the table from me. Chico had finished his banana, and was straddling his chair like a cowboy.

"When are you going to see Milton again?" he asked.

"She told you about him?"

"Of course," he answered, "she tells me everything. I'm the only family she has left."

"What about her mother?" I asked. I remembered her telling me that her mother had had a picture of me back home.

"My sister is dead," he said. He showed as much emotion as if he had said that the moon was rising.

I waited for him to say something tender like "I miss her," or, "she lived a good life," or, "she was my baby sister."

He said none of these things. When he finally spoke again, he said, "When are you going to see Milton?"

"This afternoon," I answered.

"Good," he said. Then nodding his head in Chico's direction, he said, "I want my man here to go with you to get some pictures. Don't worry, Milton won't even know he's there."

I gave him the address of Sally's up on north Broadway, then finished my sticky rice.

Milton was animated when we met up later that day.

"We have a contact," he said. "Bruce found her. Her name is Beverly Zajac."

I wasn't quite sure how to process this information. I didn't know her relationship to Avel. Was I supposed to go knock on her door?

Was I supposed to call her? What was I supposed to say to her? What was I supposed to ask her? "Cool," I said. "So what's the next step?"

"This is a slam dunk," Milton said. "Turns out that she and this dude used to have a thing together. Now, he's raising her baby."

"Oh," I said.

"It gets better," he continued. "She walked out on both of them right after the kid was born, but now she wants to see her baby."

"But let me guess," I said. "She's afraid the old boyfriend will be pissed."

"Bingo! And that's where you come in. You smooth the way for her to see the kid, and she leads you to the mark. Easy as child's play."

All at once, Milton stiffened up. Then he relaxed a little, and took a step to his right.

"So, where can I find her?" I asked.

"Don't move," he said.

"What?"

"Don't move. Don't turn around. Somebody is across the street taking pictures of us."

In retrospect, I should have said, "What the fuck?" But I didn't. Instead, I took half a breath, and froze.

Milton looked at me. "You bastard," he said. "You set me up."

Again, I should have said, "What the fuck?" Again, I didn't.

Stepping away from me, and still using my body to shield him from the lens, he said, "You on your own, Jones." Then he turned abruptly, and darted around the corner.

I stood for a moment conflicted. Should I have told him about Chico? I walked the few paces to the corner, and looked for Milton down the street. He was already gone.

Now *I* was pissed. I spun around expecting to see Chico with his camera pointed in my direction, but he was gone, too. A CTA bus roared in front of me, blocking my view of the area for about two seconds. When it passed, nothing had changed. The tavern, the grocery store and the tattoo parlor were still there. As I headed back to the car, I wondered whether or not I could find Beverly Zajac by myself.

"Your man messed up," I said walking into the house.

Master Yuen already knew what I was talking about. "We have some good pictures," he answered.

"Yeah," I said, "of the back of my head."

He handed me an 8.5 by 11 color print. It wasn't the back of my head, and it wasn't Milton. It was somebody crouched behind the brick facing on the roof of the building that housed the tattoo parlor. He was taking a picture of something across the street. Then it struck me. Chico got a shot of someone who was taking a picture of me and Milton across the street!

"Who is this?" I asked.

"We don't know."

"Milton was right," I said. "Somebody set him up."

"Maybe somebody set *you* up," he said.

This was getting too complicated. Besides the people in this house, the only person who knew I met with him there was him. If he was the one who set me up, he didn't have to let me know what was going down. On the other hand, by telling me about it, he had established a solid ground for plausible deniability should the pictures ever come to light.

"Yeah," I said. "Maybe somebody *did* set me up."

I didn't tell this to Master Yuen, but now I couldn't know who to trust. From my vantage point, it could have as easily been him or Chico as it could have been Milton. And that's only assuming that I was the mark here. It could still be that Milton was the mark.

That night, the same truck drove into the alley behind the house. The same little man with the huge beer belly rolled out of the cab, and waddled to the front of the truck. This time, I took delivery. He paid me $15,000 in cash for 30 people, fifteen women and fifteen men.

Unlike the first group, this group made themselves right at home. I reckoned a couple of them had done this before. They checked out the whole apartment, then broke up into smaller groups for sleeping arrangements in each room. By the time I left, those who had blankets were staking out spaces to spread them out. Those who didn't were simply huddling in a corner somewhere. These folks must have been really tired.

Sex that night was like a continuation of the night before. Jiqin couldn't wait to get me inside her, and I couldn't wait to oblige. She writhed as I pushed into her deeper with each stoke. Damn! If I had known she was going to be this good, I would have told her that I loved her a long time ago.

IX

It was Miss Abbey who told me the rest of what I learned about Cop Buck. Of course, she didn't call him that. She called him Beaman. And every time she mentioned his name, her face would slide into a different expression. Sometimes it reflected sadness, sometimes anger, sometimes melancholy.

Finally one day, she came out with it. "I hate the man," she said. "He destroyed my life."

She had that far-off look in her eyes. She wasn't really talking to me. She was simply venting her regrets. But I think she felt more at ease venting with me around, because she was reasonably certain that I didn't understand her musings anyway. She was right. At the time, I didn't.

"Beaman was a thug," she said. "I should have told Faith's daddy what Beaman was doing to his little girl out behind the shed of an evening."

"What was he doing?" I asked.

She came back to the moment briefly, and looked at me. Then, remembering that I was young and didn't understand the 'behind the shed' reference, she said, "He was taking advantage of her innocense."

"Huh?" I said.

She leaned over a little, and lowered her voice, "He was sticking his thing in her." She sat back in her chair now assured that she had made everything crystal clear. I was about to ask, what thing? But she blinked a couple of times, and was back into her story. "And the funny thing about it," she said, "he wasn't doing it for her. He was doing it because of the danger. He knew that he was risking his life, and he liked it."

"What was dangerous about sticking his thing in her?" I asked. I phrased the question as if I knew what she was talking about. My hope was that she would give some more details about what she meant.

"Niggers weren't supposed to fuck southern white girls," she said. "Not in Arkansas." The words must have had an acerbic taste, because she stopped talking for a moment as she worked her tongue around in her mouth to clear the bile. Then she looked at me, and said, "I'm sorry. I shouldn't have used that word around you."

I was young. I didn't even know why she was apologizing.

"Faith was a Carpenter," she continued, "and the Carpenters ran that little town."

"Like Jesus was a carpenter?" I asked.

"No, honey," she said, smiling broadly, "her maiden name was Carpenter." Then the smile faded slowly. "Thad Carpenter would have hung Beaman from the tallest pine in the county."

"So, why didn't you tell him?" I asked.

"Because in Thad Carpenter's eyes, I was trash."

"Why?"

She paused for a moment, then went on, "I loved Faith like a sister. At least, that's what I used to tell her. We grew up together, went to school together, everything. But in truth, as we got older, my love for Faith changed."

"What? You didn't love her anymore?"

"No, it changed in a different way. It changed from sister love to woman love, and Thad Carpenter saw it. He never said anything, but he began filling Faith's time with chores so she couldn't be with me. Thad never told Faith about me, because he didn't want to discuss such a worldly topic with his young daughter. I was so hurt. Faith was, too, but for a different reason."

"So, what did you do?" I asked.

"Nothing," she answered. "There was nothing I *could* do." She paused for a long moment, then slowly shook her head. "That's when Beaman moved in on her. He used to sweep up around the Carpenter's store, and do odd jobs. Nobody really knew where he came from. He just showed up in town one day looking for work. It was rumored among the Negroes that he had run away from something he had done in Alabama or Mississippi or Georgia or somewhere. It was never really clear. And to tell the truth, she was the one who made the first move. She asked him if the rumors were true. She always was too curious for her own good."

"Well, were they?" I asked.

"He told her they were, but to not tell anyone. And oh, she liked that. Nothing appealed to her more than knowing something her daddy didn't know."

"So, what did he say he did?"

"He said he killed a man in a knife fight." She paused again, then said, "A white man."

I didn't know what difference that made, and was looking for a graceful way to phrase the question. Apparently, she saw my dilemma.

"Negroes don't kill white people in this country. Especially, not in the South. White folks hang them if they do."

For some reason, I felt really glad to be living in Chicago, just in case.

"What's wrong with white folks?" I asked. "They want to hang somebody for every little thing."

"Murder is not a little thing," she said.

"Would they hang him if he killed a Negro?"

"Probably not," she answered.

"I don't get it," I said. "They would hang him if he stuck his thing in a white girl, but not if he killed a Negro. That's not fair."

She exhaled sharply through her nose. "Life's not fair," she said. "Life's not fair."

"So, when did he stick his thing in her?" I blurted out.

"Oh, that took a few weeks," she said. "After he confirmed that the rumors were true, she was drawn to him like a moth to a flame. He tried to avoid her, because he knew the risk. But after a while, when her daddy wasn't looking, she would brush up against him accidently on purpose. He would pretend to not notice, but she wouldn't be ignored. One day, she brushed up against him, and he put his broom down and walked out back behind the tool shed. She followed him."

I hated it when she paused like that. "So, what happened next?" I asked.

"He grabbed her up in his arms, straddled a sawhorse, rested her butt on that sawhorse, and fucked her. That's what happened next."

"You mean he stuck his thing in her?" I asked.

The far-away look was gone for now. "Yes," she answered. "He stuck his thing in her."

I still wasn't satisfied. I didn't want to ask the question, because I had been leading on that I knew what she was talking about. I looked around at things in the kitchen searching for a way to ask without appearing to be asking, the coiled metal handles on the old stove, the slats of wood making up the floor. Then it hit me. "What did his thing look like?" I asked.

Miss Abbey looked at me. Her expression was so . . . I don't know what it was. But I couldn't look at her. I had to look away.

"His thing looked like your thing," she said.

"My thing?! I've got a thing?!"

"Yes," she answered. "The thing you pee-pee with."

"That thing?!"

"Yes."

"He stuck *that* in her?!"

"Yes."

"Why would she let him do *that*?"

"Because it feels good," she answered.

"Suppose he had peed in her? No wonder they wanted to hang him. That's nasty!"

She laughed at me. I laughed because she laughed. When the follow-up question flashed in my mind, I stopped laughing.

"Where did he put it?" I asked.

Miss Abbey stopped laughing, too. She pointed to her lap. All I saw was the pale yellow flowers on her dress.

"What's that?" I asked.

"He stuck it between her legs," she answered.

"Oh," I said. "That's different. That's not actually *in* her."

"It's in her," she said.

"How is it in her? There's nothing there. I've seen my mother with no clothes on. There's nothing there."

She thought for a moment. "You've never seen one, have you?"

"Seen what?"

She thought again, then said, "I'm going to show you something, but you must promise never to tell anyone that I did."

"What?" I asked.

"Do you promise?"

"Yes, I promise."

"Cross your heart and hope to die."

"Yes."

"Do it," she said.

"Do what?"

"Cross your heart and hope to die."

So I did. I crossed my heart and hoped that I would die if I ever revealed that she showed me whatever it was that she was about to show me.

"Okay," she said, "stand here."

She positioned me right in front of her knees. She pulled the hem of her dress up along her thighs and gathered it around her waist. She shifted her bottom from side to side to get it all the way up in back as well.

Her knees and thighs were pasty white. I had never seen this much of a white person before. She wore white cotton panties. She hesitated a moment, then slipped her fingers inside the leg opening, and pulled the material to one side. There was a mat of grizzled hair.

"All I see is hair," I said.

She fumbled around moving hair from side to side, but it always flipped back into place.

"There's nothing there but hair," I said.

"Okay," she said. "Let's do this right."

She moved me back a pace or so, then stood up. Her dress fell back into place around her calves. She reached under her dress and pulled her panties all the way down. She stepped completely out of them. She gathered the hem around her waist again, then sat back down on the front edge of her chair. She leaned back, pulled her knees up to her chest, and spread her legs as far as she could. She positioned one hand on each side of the patch of hair, and pulled the patch apart. There it was.

"Oh," I said.

"Oh," she mimicked.

I leaned forward to get a closer look. I was still standing that pace or so back.

"You can come closer," she said.

I was afraid. At the same time, I was fascinated. I stepped forward one pace, then another, then another, all the while bending closer and closer to it. I was transfixed. I couldn't take my eyes away. As I got closer, I could smell it. I had never smelled anything like this before, and it affected me in a strange way. My breathing became deeper as I tried to pull more of the aroma into my nostrils.

"Can I touch it?" I asked.

"No!" she said sharply.

"I see it, but I don't actually see a hole that you could put anything in."

"Give me your hand," she said.

My hand was small compared to hers. She took my index and middle fingers, and guided them across the smooth pink flesh until magically they pushed the tissue apart and disappeared into her body. She was deliciously warm inside. I was trying to understand what had just happened when she pulled them out and ordered me to go wash my hands. I wanted to explain that I wanted to explore this thing further, but she stood up and pulled her panties back on. By the time I had gathered my thoughts together, she was standing up brushing her dress back into place with short downward strokes.

"Go wash your hands."

I walked slowly into the bathroom and closed the door. I wanted to smell her scent on my fingers, but I didn't want her to see me do it. I inhaled deeply several times. I wanted to taste it, but I heard myself telling her "that's nasty." It didn't have the same ring now as it did then. All of a sudden, nasty didn't mean nasty the way it used to.

I washed my hands and dried them. I smelled my fingers again, but her scent was gone. I smelled of Lifeboy.

Anxious to talk about what we had just done, I dashed back out into the kitchen. She was sitting there with her hands folded in her lap. I took a breath preparatory to firing off multiple questions when I noticed Miss Blue sitting in my chair.

"So," Miss Blue asked, "did you guys have a good time together?"

I nodded yes.

"So, tell me what you did."

I shrugged. "We talked," I said.

"Is that all?" she asked. "Didn't you do anything fun or interesting?"

I shrugged again.

After a long moment, Miss Abbey said, "It's getting late, Faith. I've got to go."

Miss Blue saw her out, then came back to the kitchen.

"Your mother should be here soon to pick you up," she said. "I know you must be tired. Sue can rattle on."

She tilted her head to an angle and sniffed. "What is that smell?" she asked.

I shrugged yet again.

Mama picked me up shortly thereafter, and we walked home. All the while though, my thoughts were on Miss Abbey's scent and the feel of her warm, moist flesh.

X

I got up early the next morning. I needed to talk to Milton. I needed to look him in the eye as I asked him about who might have been taking pictures of us yesterday. I hoped he would be outside Sally's early trying to get some moving work. I approached Sally's from the other side of the street. I wanted to see the scene in front of the place before I actually walked into it. I didn't want any surprises.

From my vantage point, I could see three men milling around the entrance. They were standing close, almost huddled together as if they were whispering something among themselves. I suspected they were looking for work. Sure enough, within five minutes, a minivan drove up, and, after some preliminary talk, two of them got into the van. As the van pulled off, the third man headed back into the building. Checking the traffic, I loped across the street. As I approached the building, I decided to go inside and ask for Milton rather than milling around outside waiting. I yanked the door open, and a woman on the other side about to lean onto it to get out came crashing into my chest. Both of us went sprawling to the ground. Well, almost. I managed to catch myself with one hand on the ground and a twist of my body. The woman wasn't so lucky. She went face first into the concrete sidewalk.

"Goddamn you," she said, rolling over, then heaving her body into a seated position in the middle of the pavement.

She was in bad shape. Her forehead was cut and bleeding into her eye. A half inch round of flesh was missing from the side of her nose. The shoulder of her jacket was scraped where it rubbed across the concrete, and her knee was bleeding from a four inch hole in her stocking.

"I am so sorry," I said.

"Fuck you," she said. Then she continued, "Help me up."

I grabbed her by the arm and tugged. She weighted a ton! I was in shape, and it was all I could do to keep from being pulled to the ground with her. The problem was that she was trying to get up while favoring the leg with the busted up knee. She was sort of trying to hop onto her good leg, but she weighted too much. The hop ended up being nothing more than a flinch that yanked down on me. Eventually, realizing this approach wasn't going to work, she gingerly brought the injured leg into play. She grunted and groaned and finally heaved herself into an almost upright position. She leaned on me to avoid putting too much weight onto her bad leg.

I angled us around to head for the door. I wanted to get her back inside so that she could sit down.

"No!" she said. "I'm not going back in there."

"Why?" I asked. "We can get help in there."

"Fuck them," she said. "I want a drink."

"A drink! You need to get some help."

"I got help," she said. "I got you. Get me a cab, and let's find a tavern."

"I can't go to a bar. I'm trying to meet somebody here."

"You *did* meet somebody. You met me. And the least you can do is buy me a fucking drink."

The only bar I knew was the one over on Broadway at Lawrence, where the brother wanted me to confirm the vitamin content of orange juice. The same barmaid was there.

"Hey, boo," she said, smiling that smile that pulled the corners of her mouth down. Then she saw that I was with someone and that the someone was bleeding. "Oh, my God," she said, "What happened?" She reached under the bar for something, then came out of her work area to the table beside the door where I was helping this woman ease into a chair. "What happened?" the barmaid asked again, "Did this fool hurt you?" There was mock indignation in her voice again.

"No," the answer came, "I fell. I am such a klutz sometimes."

The something the barmaid had grabbed from behind the bar was a first-aid kit. "Here," she said, "let me take a look at that." She tore open a packet that contained a miniature moist towel of some sort, then began dabbing at the cut over the woman's eye. "My name is Joyce," she said. "What's yours?"

"Bev."

It was a good thing that I was sitting on the side of her with the cut eye. Otherwise, she might have seen me flinch. This was Beverly Zajac. I just knew it.

"Okay, Bev," Joyce said, "here's the deal. This cut could use a couple of stitches."

"I got no money for stitches," Bev said. "Can you just throw a Band-Aid over it?"

"Sure, honey, I can do that. But it will probably leave a scar."

Joyce put a bandage on Bev's eyebrow, then used a fresh towel on Bev's nose. "This is just a scrape," she said. "Now, let's see that knee."

Bev moved her meaty leg over so that Joyce could look at it.

"Make this clown buy you some more stockings," Joyce said dabbing at Bev's knee.

"He's going to buy me a drink instead," Bev countered. "Something expensive."

"I got Champaign in the basement."

"I hate Champaign. Just make it a Cosmo."

"This knee will probably be stiff for a little while, but I think it'll be all right. You should have it X-rayed."

"Just make it a double Cosmo," Bev said. "The booze will fix whatever is wrong with me."

Joyce cleaned up the mess from the kit, and returned to the bar. "What are *you* going to have, slick?"

"I'll take a Shirley Temple," I said.

"Now, that's what I call a real *man's* drink," Joyce chortled.

Joyce served our drinks, and I paid her. I gave her a ten dollar tip. What she did for Bev was above and beyond. She thanked me, then disappeared somewhere in the back.

"So who did you think you were supposed to meet at Sally's?"

"That's not important," I answered.

"I know everybody there," she said.

"His name is Milton."

"Reverend Milton? You know Reverend Milton?"

"Well," I answered cautiously, "yeah."

"Fuck me," she said, "of all the assholes in the world to run into, I pick a friend of the biggest asshole on earth."

"What did I do to be an asshole?!"

"You mentioned asshole's name, that's what you did."

"All I said was Milton."

"See, you did it again."

"Did what?"

"That fool owes me money."

"Who?"

"It's a good thing I ran into you. I saved you the heartache of missing out on his company."

"Oh?" I said.

"He wasn't there. Hiding from me, no doubt."

"You shouldn't have loaned him money."

"I didn't. He was supposed to pay me for some information I gave him."

"Maybe you should have kept it to yourself," I said. "How much does he owe you?"

"Fifty bucks."

"Must have been some good information."

"He thought so."

"So what was the information? The next winner at Sportsman's Park?"

"It wouldn't interest you."

"Try me," I said.

"You got the fifty dollars?" she asked.

"I might."

"I might ain't good enough."

"I got it."

"Let's see it."

"I got it," I said again. "What's the information about?"

"A cop. My ex-boyfriend."

I reached into my pocket and fished out the money. A twenty, a ten, three fives and five singles.

"So how did Milton even find you?" I asked.

"That's a long story."

"Give me the short version."

"Through a mutual acquaintance named Bruce."

"Bruce was his buddy."

"Bruce was my probation officer."

"What were you in for?"

"Hooking."

"First time?"

"Yeah, and last time."

"So what did Milton want to know?"

"Reverend Milton wanted to know who killed that kid. What was his name?"

"Pemberly," I answered.

"Right. Marcus Pemberly. He wanted to know who killed him."

"Did he say *why* he wanted to know?"

"No. He simply offered fifty bucks for the name."

Now my interest was really piqued. "How did you come to know who did it?" I asked.

She hesitated, then gulped down her Cosmo. She motioned to the glass. I nodded to Joyce who was now back at her station behind the bar. Joyce mixed up a fresh batch, and served it up.

"I can't tell you any more," Bev said.

"You haven't told me anything, yet."

"I'll give you what Milton wanted. The guy's name is Avel."

"I know his name," I said. "I need to know more than that."

Bev knocked back the second Cosmo, and thumped the glass on the table. I nodded to Joyce again. I raised three fingers indicating to make it a triple.

"I can't," Bev said. "I can't. I can't. I can't."

Joyce served up the new batch of liquor. Bev reached for it, but I moved the glass just beyond her reach. She leaned forward more, and

I moved the glass a little more.

"I'm not telling you shit without this drink," she said.

I pushed the glass with one finger to just within her reach. She lunged for it and drained half the glass. She sat back and took several deep breaths through her nose.

"Talk to me," I said.

She sat breathing deeply. Then she said, "If I tell you, he'll kill me."

"You've already given me his name."

"That's nothing," she said. "I could give you his name, address, phone number and schedule. He wouldn't care about that."

"There *is* nothing else," I said. "That's all I need."

"Yes, but that's not all there is."

"Meaning?"

She sat with her lips pressed tight together. Then she turned her head slowly from side to side. "I don't want to die," she said. She scribbled Avel's address on a napkin, finished her drink, then staggered out of her seat. She limped because of her leg injury, and the Cosmos were beginning to take their toll. She hugged the wall for stability as she headed for the door. "Don't call me. I'll call you," she said reaching for the handle.

"I'm going to have to tell him who gave me his name," I said.

"So tell him."

"If I do, he won't likely let you see your baby."

She stopped cold. "You bastard," she said. "You fucking bastard."

"Wasn't that part of the deal you cut with Milton? You give him the name, and we smooth the way for you to see your kid?"

"I kept my end of the deal," she said.

"I know," I said. "And you've done a good job. But the deal has changed."

"That's not fair," she protested.

"I know, but sometimes life is like that."

"What do you want me to do?"

"I want you to talk to me," I said. "I want you to tell me about Avel."

She struggled back to her seat. With one finger, she eased her glass in my direction. I signaled Joyce.

"Avel works for the Heritance Foundation," she said.

"Avel is a cop," I corrected. "He works for the city."

"He gets paid by the city," she said. "He *works* for the foundation."

"I'm confused," I said.

"I'll explain. The Heritance Foundation was formed in the late sixties by ex-members of the Ku Klux Klan. They gathered in Dearborn, Michigan, and decided that the methods used by the Klan were the Klan's undoing. They decided that the Klan had been too public, too in-your-face despite the fact that everyone kept their faces covered."

Joyce served the new Cosmo.

Bev's speech was beginning to slur because of what she had already had, but she took another long swallow. Some of the fluid ran from the glass down both sides of her chin. She wiped her mouth with the back of her hand. "The Klan had been secretive, but they decided that the true intention of the foundation would be invisible. Even the name would sound all-American. And rather than work outside the system as the Klan had done, they would use the system. They did their homework. They remembered how the state of Georgia had used the law to prevent Black people from voting. Georgia simply mandated that felons couldn't vote, then proceeded to make every law that Black people broke a felony. After a while, white people ran the state with no input from the large black community. The founders of the Heritance Foundation decided to expand that concept, and to implement it nationwide."

She took a sip of her drink, rolled it around in her mouth, then swallowed. "So now," she continued, "they hire conservative eggheads who do nothing but sit around and think up policies, policies that make it impossible for Black people to get ahead in society. One of their primary goals is the elimination of the federal Social Security program. Black people depend almost exclusively on Social Security for support when they retire. Dismantling that program would decimate the Black community. So what do they do? They issue position papers claiming to support the concepts of self-reliance and self-determination and self-responsibility. They make Social Security sound like welfare. Cowboy politicians in Washington pick up on the notion, and before long, folks are talking about Social Security being bad for the country."

"Social Security is self-supporting," I said.

"I know that, and you know that. But they tell people that Social Security is paid for from the general revenue fund. It's a flat out lie, but most people don't know the difference. They don't know that Congress borrowed money from Social Security years ago when Social Security had a huge surplus. That surplus is gone now because Congress spent it. Now, Congress is having to pay Social Security back, and it looks like welfare."

"Where do they get their funding?" I asked.

"Their goal is to make their policies the guiding principles of American politics."

"Where do they get their funding?" I asked again.

"Corporations," she answered. "Large corporations spend millions of dollars annually supporting the Heritance Foundation. It's a cycle. Large corporations pay the Foundation to announce these right-wing policies, then the same corporations support the campaigns of politicians who support these policies in government. The Heritance Foundation has an enormous influence on the policies being adopted by right-wing politicians, and Avel works for *them*."

"In what capacity?" I asked.

"The Foundation recruits people. It recruits young white men, indoctrinates them with conservative dogma, then encourages them to join police forces across the nation, especially in big cities. Why do you suppose there aren't any white gang bangers? They're all cops. As cops, they get to kill Black and brown men, and never be held accountable. That or charge them with felonies that end up stripping them of their voting rights. Cops *never* go to prison."

I thought about Milton. Cops go to prison if they are Black, and are trying to protect the community.

"Did you ever tell Milton this?" I asked.

"No," she answered. "Why should I?"

"He would give you a week's pay for this information."

"And that ain't even all," she said.

"There's more?"

"Oh, there's lots more. Why do you suppose there are so many abortion clinics in the African American community?"

"The ones under Planet Parenthood?"

"That's the one! Their slogan is 'A Whole New World.' What do you think that means?"

"I don't know," I answered. "A planet free of struggling single moms?"

"No! It means a planet free of Black people. Planet Parenthood is an extermination program conceived, implemented and funded by the Heritance Foundation. Black babies make up the lion's share of abortion deaths. 2000 a year!"

"What?!"

"That's right, 2000 Black babies get aborted every year, year after year after year. And that was Planet Parenthood's goal. They want to build a thoroughbred race of people on earth. All white; all blonde; all blue-eyed. The Nazis have returned, and they have set up shop in America."

For the first time since starting this project, I began to doubt its importance. Maybe Milton had been right. Avel was only a foot soldier. Maybe I should just pass him up. On the other hand, foot soldiers can and do wreak havoc in the community, and these assholes need to be sent a message. Besides, I had to start somewhere.

"We can stop him," I said. I kept my voice low so Joyce wouldn't hear me.

"How? He's a cop. He's protected by the badge."

"Badges don't protect a fucking thing," I said. "Give me your number. When the time is right, I'll contact you."

"What about my baby?" she asked.

"Tell me about that," I answered.

She told me everything. I guess I had expected her to tell the story in a way that cast her in a favorable light. But she didn't. She was a flaky ass bitch, and she knew it. And that's the way she told the story. The way she told it, Avel became a sympathetic character. I began to doubt that he was a suitable mark. I began to doubt that he should be killed. Then I recalled what she had just told me about the Heritance Foundation.

"Okay," I said after her narrative, "I want to help you get your baby back."

"You can do that?!" she asked.

"I can try." I pulled the crumpled piece of paper that Milton had given me with Tina Pemberly's information on it. I turned it over, and told Bev to write her telephone number on it.

"What do I have to do?" she asked while scribbling her number.

"I'll call you and tell you what to do," I said. "Don't worry. You'll see your baby."

I could hear Milton telling his magician story. "Their only reward is that of the fool," he had said. His words cut me more deeply now than they did then. The Heritance Foundation was playing all of us for fools, and getting away with it. It was time for this "fool" to get a different reward. I gave Bev the fifty dollars, paid for the drinks, and left.

I had wanted to head back to the house. But something told me to check in front of Sally's before I left the north side. Milton was there standing by the door with his hands stuffed into his pockets. It was as if he was just standing there waiting for me.

He didn't see me as I approached, because he was caught up staring at the flashing blue lights of a passing squadral in the opposite direction. But when I called his name to get his attention, he didn't act surprised. He started in as if nothing had happened. "Think about this," he said, "What do Bob Marley and Tupac Shakur have in common?"

"Both brothers," I answered, "both musicians. What are you getting at?"

"Both died young?"

"Both died young. Where you going with this?"

"Both murdered," he said.

"One murdered," I corrected, "Marley died of cancer."

"They were both murdered," he said, "by the CIA."

"Milton," I said, "you've got your facts wrong. Marley died of cancer."

"That's what it was made to look like," he said.

"Look, he either had cancer or he didn't. There is no middle ground here."

"What kind of cancer did he have?" he asked.

"I don't know of what. What difference does *that* make?"

"It makes all the difference in the world."

"You're baiting me, aren't you? Okay, I'll bite. What kind of cancer did Bob Marley have?"

"I have no idea."

"So what's your point?"

"My point is that nobody has any idea."

"C'mon, man, cancer is cancer."

"No," he asserted, "cancer is *not* cancer. Cancer is cervical cancer. Cancer is bone cancer. Cancer is cancer of the brain."

"You're losing me here."

"Cancer starts in one spot, then metastasises."

"Okay," I said.

"Except in Marley's case it was everywhere all at once."

"That's not possible," I said. "It had to start somewhere."

"Yeah," Milton said, "it started in a CIA laboratory."

"Come on, man! You're doing it again."

"Doing what?"

"Jumping to conclusions where no jump is warranted."

"But the jump *is* warranted."

"You cannot be serious!"

"Why not?"

"How did they get it into his body? Telepathy?"

"They injected it into him."

"When? How?"

"Marley had hurt his toe playing soccer about a year earlier. He went to the doctor to have it treated, and they gave him a shot in his toe."

"The cancer shot." I couldn't believe Milton was making such an idiotic claim.

"Right," he said, "the cancer shot."

"And how did they hook it up? Were all the doctors in the world supplied with cancer-causing serum just in case Marley stopped in?"

"They knew who his doctor was, I guess."

"Okay," I said. "But why? Why him?"

"He had become too dangerous."

"The man was a musician! How dangerous could that have been?"

"Have you listened to his music? He sang about revolution. He sang about getting out of slavery. And people were listening. He was getting a worldwide following."

"They were only songs, for Christ sake."

"Bob Dylan wrote 'The Times They Are A-Changin'', and changed the planet. He was like Moses leading the Jews out of Egypt. In fact, if the CIA had had any idea of the impact that song would have on American culture, they would have shot *his* ass. They didn't want Marley's songs to do the same thing."

"And I guess they killed Tupac for the same reason?"

"Damn right! His following was getting too big, too. Men were writing him from prison asking him to tell them what to do. Tupac's power was awesome. He was considered to be the single most powerful Black man in America. Maybe even the world." He paused for a moment, then said, "But you know what?"

"What?" I answered.

"Their strategy won't save them. They think the movement needs a Moses. It don't. Every man walking is a Moses all by himself. The genie is already out the bottle, and when the time comes, we *will* win."

Milton stood nodding for a few moments staring at the sidewalk. He stood staring at the exact spot where Bev had earlier crashed like a sandbag.

"Look," I said, "we need to talk about yesterday."

"Nothing to talk about," he said.

"I didn't set you up."

He looked me straight in the eye. "I don't believe you," he said, "but I don't care." He lowered his eyes. "I'm not going back inside no matter what you do or what anybody else does. Now, get the fuck away from here." He jerked his head in the direction I would have to leave. As I walked away, he was still staring at the Bev crash site.

"Don't come back," he shouted from behind me. "I can't afford to give you any more help."

It crossed my mind to show him the picture of the guy on the roof taking pictures. But that would only serve to confirm his suspicions about me. Someone working for me, after all, had taken *that* picture. I had to let it go. Besides, I had already gotten everything I needed and more from Bev. I didn't bother to look back. He was right. This epoch was over.

XI

"I'm pregnant."

"What?"

"I'm pregnant."

"How did that happen? I mean, I know how it happened, but . . ."

"I'm going to get an abortion."

"No!" I said, "Don't do that."

"Why not?" She said, "You said so yourself. We can't get married."

"I know, I know. But I need to think."

"About what?"

"Are you sure?"

"I'm sure," she said, "I stopped in at a clinic today."

"I mean are you sure it's . . .?"

"Yours?" She finished the sentence for me. She made that sucking sound with her teeth that people make when they see a grown-ass man do something that only a teenager would do like ask his girlfriend, the one he's been fucking non-stop for weeks with no protection just like he didn't know this was how babies got made, whether she was sure it was his. "Yes, Jay," she said, "I am carrying . . . your baby."

"That's not what I meant. I mean . . . I mean . . ."

She walked out of the room and slammed the door. I hesitated a moment, then ran after her. When I opened the door, she was still standing just on the other side, her back to me. I slid my arms around her waist, and pulled her close to me. I slid my hand under her t-shirt, and ran it back and forth across both her little breasts. They felt warm and soft.

"We can do this," I said.

"Do what?" she responded, pulling away from me. "I'm not having this baby."

"Why not?"

"I'm just not is all."

My feelings were hurt, but I tried to control the quaver in my voice. "It's my baby, too," I said.

"Yeah, but you don't have to push it out and raise it. I have to do that, and I'm not sure I'm ready."

She stood there in the same tattered grey University of Wisconsin t-shirt and long denim skirt she had worn the day I woke up in her uncle's house. I remembered the three INS agents who broke in on us in the upstairs bedroom. They were dressed in cheap, ill-fitting suits, one grey, one blue, one brown. The one in grey was tall; his suit was too short. The one in blue was fat; his suit was too snug. The one in brown was small; his suit was baggy. Jiqin had pleaded with me to pretend the house belonged to me. The expression on her delicate round and flat face then and the expression on it now were the same. The same cow-brown eyes looking at me from beneath the hood of her lids, the same full lips squeezed tight together, the same flat little nose with the nostrils flexing as if it had a tiny heart beat of its very own. Back then, I knew what she wanted. This time, I wasn't sure.

"What do you want me to do?" I asked.

She paused a moment, then answered, "Nothing. I'll take care of it."

She turned slowly to head downstairs.

"I'll raise it," I blurted out.

She stopped.

"You have it. I'll raise it."

She turned towards me again. Her eyes began to well up with water.

"What?" I asked, "What did I do?"

Now she was crying for they ass. She flung her arms around my neck, and sobbed in my ear.

"I love you so much," she said.

"What?" I asked again. "What did I say?"

She didn't answer. But I just sort of figured that she had changed her mind about killing the baby.

What is it with women and them wanting you to know what they want without them telling you what it is? Ida had been like that when *she* was pregnant. They change. They start acting all funny. Not that they don't act funny all along. They just act more funny when they get pregnant. They think differently and their scent changes. And just at that moment, I noticed that Jiqin's scent was different. She had that same pregnant smell.

"Does your uncle know?" I asked.

She pulled away and became all matter-of-fact. She sniffed and mopped her eyes with the backs of her hands.

"No," she said, "but I can tell him today, and tell him that we'll get married as soon as we get this immigration thing cleared up." She took a couple of quick steps towards the stairs, then turned and took those same steps back towards me, then turned again back towards the stairs. "We need baby stuff, diapers and wipes and toys. Nobody's going to give us a baby shower."

"We don't know anybody," I said.

"My point exactly," she answered. Then she stopped. "Did you see Milton today?"

I wasn't sure how it was that having this baby reminded her of Milton, but I went along with the flow.

"Yeah," I answered. "I saw him."

"So, what did he say?"

"About what?"

"About anything." She had that what-the-fuck-do-you-mean-about-what sound in her voice.

"He wants me to stay away from him."

"He does?" She was genuinely surprised.

"He thinks I brought the fuzz around."

"Did you show him the pictures?"

"No," I answered. "There was no way to show him without letting him know that I had someone else there taking pictures."

She thought for a moment, then said, "We need to watch him. Something isn't right."

She went downstairs to tell her uncle about the baby, but I decided to stay put. I needed to think. Too many things were happening too fast, and I needed to get my head straight.

Maybe it's in the genes. Maybe it's something humans carry from before we were humans, from a time when bearing offspring could mean the success or failure of the species. I couldn't put my finger on it, but all of a sudden, I wanted to be safe. I wanted to make sure nothing happened to Jiqin. I wanted to make sure nothing happened to me so that I could be around to make sure nothing happened to her. I was beginning to doubt the wisdom of my chosen course of action. The life of an assassin isn't one one brings a family into unless one has to. I wasn't sure I had to. I had other options. I had safe options. I could drive something or other. A bus, a truck. I could work at that paper cup factory over on 75th Street. Then it hit me. Who the fuck was I kidding? We are who we are, and we do what we do. There are no safe options. Safety on earth is an illusion.

"Jay!" Jiqin called me from downstairs. "We don't have any ice cream."

I wasn't sure what she was getting at, so I answered, "Okay."

After a short pause, she called again, "Jay?"

"Yes?"

"I need some ice cream."

Now I got it. "Do you need pickles, too?" I asked.

"No, honey, just ice cream. Can you go get me some?"

Supermarkets are an anathema to thinking beings. Nothing is where you want it to be. The one over on Exchange Avenue was no exception. I wanted ice cream. Only ice cream. But to get to it, I had to wade through aisles of cereal and spices and detergent. At the end of the cereal aisle, I saw corn flakes. The mere seeing of the box conjured up images of me as a kid eating a bowl of corn flakes with sliced banana, sugar and milk, a meal I hadn't had in years. I picked up a box. Now, I needed a banana. As I walked back around to the produce section, I heard a fire engine roar by with its siren blaring. It was so loud, I had to stop what I was doing. It sped right by the front of the store, and everybody there looked out the front window in time enough to see its shiny, red panels and gleaming chrome railings. I redirected my attention back to the bananas, and found two that I wanted, yellow with tiny brown pin pricks.

I headed back to the ice cream cooler. As I reached in for a half-gallon carton of French Vanilla, I heard a second fire truck roar by. I couldn't see it from where I was, but the sound was unmistakable. It was the sound of a powerful diesel engine. It sounded like a freight train.

I checked out and strolled towards the car. I had to step over discarded yellow potato chip packages and empty red and white cola cans in the parking lot.

Damn! I forgot the milk. I put the cereal and bananas and ice cream in the car, and went back into the store. By the time I exited for the second time, a fire department ambulance came speeding by. This was big. I had to see what was happening.

My first instinct was to drop the bags off at home. My plan was to go home, get a camera, then follow the sound of the trucks. I turned onto 76th Street just in time to see the ambulance turning the corner towards the house. When I got to the end of the block and looked down the street, I could see where the fire was. It was my apartment building.

The whole block was clogged with fire fighting equipment and personnel. Hoses crisscrossed the street. Flashing red lights reflected off the houses on both sides. Men in long black rubber coats shouted and pointed and ran. Police squadrals with flashing blue Mars lights blocked both ends of the street. On-lookers streamed from neighboring buildings to see the spectacle up close.

Right in the middle of the intersection, I jammed the car into park, and flung open the door. As I ran towards the house, a cop ran at me from my left. He probably wanted me to move the car. I stiff-armed him straight in the chest, and sent him flying into a neighbors front yard. He fell over backwards into a rock garden, his cap careening into the street.

Smoke poured out of all the windows on the second floor. As I charged for the front of the building, I gave a quick glance at the on-lookers to see if anyone from the house was now standing outside. In particular, I looked for Jiqin. She wasn't there. Neither were any of the members of her family or crew. Down the gangway, I could see another crew of firemen shooting water onto the roof. The front door was already open, so I popped straight in and took the stairs two at a time. I heard somebody behind me shouting that the building was already empty, but I needed to see for myself.

It took me fewer than 60 seconds to run the length of the first floor apartment glancing into each room. They were all empty. All the doors were wide open like they had already been checked. I ran back to the front stairwell, and up to the third floor. I bypassed the second floor because the front door to that apartment was already blistering from the heat on the other side. I took a deep breath as I raced by, and held it. The smoke began to sting my eyes. I ran straight through the top floor apartment barely glancing into the rooms. Smoke from the fire on the second floor was pouring into the third floor through cracks at the floorboards. I needed to get out the back door to the open air. My body was crying for oxygen, and the floor was getting hot even through my shoes.

The air on the back porch was as bad as the air in the apartment. I had to keep holding my breath as I jumped down all eight stairs to the landing, and then jumped the next eight to the second story porch. I fell on my chest and face, and all my little remaining air was forced out. I could feel myself passing out as I crawled down the first length of stairs to the first floor. My body involuntarily drew in a breath. The air reeked, but it was breathable. I coughed and sneezed as I tumbled down the last few stairs to the first floor porch. I staggered out into the yard, out the back gate and down the alley towards the car.

I had a million questions going through my head. How could this happen in so short a time? Where was Jiqin and her crew? Was the baby okay? How did the fire start? Where was I going to stay tonight?

From the mouth of the alley, I approached the intersection where I had left the car. Not surprisingly, it wasn't there. It couldn't be far, because I hadn't been gone long enough for it to have been towed. I stepped off the curb, and walked to the exact spot where the engine of the car would have been. From there, I looked around hoping someone had simply moved it out of the way.

"Looking for something?" I heard a voice behind me.

I turned around. It was the cop who had tried to stop me from going in. He was a short fuck, dark for a white boy. His black eyebrows grew together in the middle. Twirling his cap around his left index finger, he stood with his feet shoulder-width apart. He probably thought the stance made him look powerful. I wondered if they taught him that in cop school. All I saw was an asshole inviting a swift kick to the nuts. I might have considered delivering the kick, but he was backed up by one of his buddies. He stood a pace behind him with that same wide-legged stance.

Just then, one of the firemen came running in our direction. "Mike," he called, "we need you down here."

Mike, the backup cop, turned to acknowledge the request, then asked, "You got this, Joe?"

"I got this," the short cop said. Then to me, "I asked you a question."

"I left my car here," I said.

"Oh!" His tone was one of mock surprise. "Was that your car? Somebody drove it away to be towed."

"You wouldn't know where that someone drove it, would you?

Maybe I can get there before the tow truck."

"But that somebody *wants* it to be towed."

"It isn't my car," I protested.

"Then you shouldn't have left it here."

It suddenly dawned on me that this conversation was pointless.

"You're right," I said. "My bad."

I stepped away from him, and headed across the street in the direction of the lake. He hopped around and blocked my way.

"You can't go this way," he said.

There was only one reason he wouldn't want me to go that way, and that is that the car was that way. I stepped back from him again, then broke into a dead run across the street to the next alley over. I knew I was taking a chance. Cops in Chicago think nothing about shooting a brother in the back. My hope was that the fire had drawn enough people into the street that he would think twice. It worked. He ran after me, but his legs were too short. There was no way for him to catch me. I rounded the corner of the alley heading north, and sure enough, there it was, still running. I slowed down. I reached for the door handle, but I was too late. I had underestimated shorty's speed. He got there just in time to throw his weight against the door to slam it shut. He had his nightstick drawn, and he swung it. This time, *he* was too late. I blocked his swing. I then shot the base of my palm right into his diaphragm. I visualized my energy going all the way through to his spine. Even his bullet-proof vest didn't protect him. The force of my blow lifted him off his feet, and sent him into the wall of the red brick building on the alley. His stick clattered on the pavement. As he landed, he unsnapped the strap holding his pistol in its holster. I leaped over to him, and planted the heel of my foot in the exact same spot that

I had popped him with the base of my palm. All the air in his lungs escaped from his mouth. I thought I heard one of his ribs break. He sank to his knees and slumped to the pavement.

I got in the car, and drove away up the alley.

It was sheer luck that I didn't kill someone driving the way I was. The car roared out of the mouth of the alley like a car in a movie chase scene. I turned the wheel hard to avoid careening into a parked pick-up truck, then jerked the wheel back and forth in order to keep it in the middle of the road. After another block and a half, I eased on the brake in order to slow down to a more normal rate of speed. My heart still raced. I couldn't control that. But I had to control that car. The last thing I needed was to get stopped for speeding, and another fucking cop trying to be a big shot.

As I drove, I wondered where I was going. My earlier questions about Jiqin and her uncle and crew and the fire circled endlessly in my mind. I needed a plan. I needed a direction.

I hadn't thought about it, but before I knew it, I was a half mile from Jiqin's uncle's house, the place she took me the day I got shot. I eased the car around the corner, and cruised slowly down the street looking at each house in turn to make sure I recognized the right one. My scrupulous attention to detail was unwarranted. The house was unmistakable. It was the only one on the block where the front door and livingroom window were riddled with bullet holes.

I drove a couple of miles away, then pulled to the side of the road. I needed to assess my situation. I had this car, and the clothes on my back. I needed money. I wondered if the $15,000 I collected for the last shipment had been burned up with the house. I emptied my pockets. Keys, change from the store, a handkerchief, a crumpled up piece of brown paper bag. I unfolded it. There was a phone number, an address and a name scrawled in pencil and scarcely visible against the wrinkles and folds of the paper. The graphite itself was smeared. The writing was barely legible, but I recognized it. The name was Tina Pemberly. Bev's number was on the other side.

I put the car into gear, and pulled away from the curb.

XII

I called Bev. I told her that I needed a place to stay for a few days. She was reluctant at first, but then I told her that I wanted to tell her what I needed for her to do. I guess she thought that if she said no, I wouldn't help her get her baby back.

Her address was on the north side, almost to the border with Evanston. I found a parking space, and sat with the engine running trying to figure out what I was going to say to her. I couldn't exactly tell her what I wanted. She might get the right idea, and shrink from me in terror. Murder wasn't exactly everybody's idea of socially acceptable behavior. On the other hand, I couldn't simply knock on her door and expect to make small talk. I needed some kind of plan that I could offer her.

Sitting there as I was, I couldn't help but notice the number of Black people on this block. This block looked a lot like my block on the south side, graffiti on the mail box, parked cars with shiny, wishbone rims, a beer can resting on the curb across the street. I didn't even know Black folks lived this far north in Chicago. Then I wondered what Bev was doing on this block. She had to be the only white person here. Maybe she had a terminal case of jungle fever. She was, after all, looking for Milton when I met her. Maybe there was more between them than fifty dollars for some requested information.

I tried to imagine Milton with a woman. He had always seemed to be so asexual. Maybe that's because he was a man, and men see other men as asexual. But more than asexual, Milton had always seemed to be vulnerable, someone a woman would want to mother, but not give pussy to.

I decided there was no reason to sit in the car hoping for inspiration to strike. I cut the engine and headed for her building.

"Here's what I'll do," she said letting me into her apartment.

She lived in a studio, and the girl was a pig. Clothes were strewn everywhere, on chairs, on tables, on the floor. It's like she walked in taking clothes off, and let them drop on the spot. She couldn't have had anything in the closets. It was all out in plain sight. And there were papers, stacks, sheets, pieces, interleaved with the clothes. Some of it was projects she was organizing. Some were notes to herself. Buy coffee. Stop drinking coffee. Kick Milton's ass. And some were just there for no obvious reason.

"I'll call him, and invite him over here," she said. "That way, you'll be able to ask him anything you want."

"No," I said, "let's not do that. He might start some shit."

"I hadn't thought about that," she said. "I wouldn't want him to fuck up my apartment."

"Neither would I," I said, looking around at the clutter.

She paused for a long moment, then said, "Listen, I've been really down on my luck lately. I've made some major fuck-ups in my life."

"I'm sorry," I said. I wasn't really, but I didn't know what else to say. I had been wondering how to start a conversation with her. Maybe this was it.

"Ever since I was a kid," she continued, "I've had it rough."

I didn't want to say that I was sorry again, so I nodded my head up and down a little. It worked. She settled into a little storytelling groove.

Her father went out on a drunk one Friday when she was about three years old. When he got back that Sunday night, her mother reminded him that the rent was coming due. He shook his head, turned

109   **The Reward of the Fool**

around, and walked back out the door.

She wasn't clear about what happened to her mother, but she remembered that one day her mother was gone, too, and after spending time with various families over a period of what she guessed was about a year, she was adopted by a couple who couldn't have children of their own. According to her, they were ignorant. They knew little or nothing about raising kids, and they made it a point of reminding her of the favor they were doing her by bringing her into their family. She gave them this, though. They never bad-mouthed her birth parents. She reckoned they probably didn't know anything about them.

Shortly after getting her, however, her adoptive mother got pregnant. They bore a son of their own, so now they didn't need her. Oh, she was included in everything they did, but the new son was the center of attention. They shopped for her at thrift and second hand stores. They shopped for him at the mall. For her birthday, they enjoyed a modest cake at home. For his birthday, they visited a kid-friendly fast food chain with an indoor playground with all the rainbow-colored ping-pong balls that you could jump around in. For Christmas, she got stuff she could share with him. He simply got stuff.

"The worst was when Odell started sticking his finger in me," she said. "I guess I was about nine. At first, I didn't do anything about it. I guess I hoped he would stop. When he didn't, I told Abbey. Worst thing I could have done. She called me a liar and a whore. I wasn't even sure what a whore was. After that, it was open season on my ass. Before long, he graduated me from his finger to his cock. I stopped even resisting. I just let him do it. I guess I liked it even though I knew it was wrong.

"I didn't dare mention it to Abbey again, but I knew she knew. And she knew that I knew that she knew. That made her hate me even more. She did everything she could to make my life miserable. Like it was my fault! I did what I knew to do to stop it. I told her. The bitch! She was pissed at him, pissed at herself, and she took it out on me.

"I ran away for the first time when I was thirteen," she said. "I didn't get far, though. The cops found me a few hours later wandering the streets about a mile from the house. You can't get very far in a small town in Vermont. As long as the cops were around, they made a big show of being glad I was back safe and sound. As soon as the cop car pulled away, though, they scolded me for embarrassing them. I failed a couple of more times, but by sixteen, I made it west to Chicago. I haven't looked back since."

"So how long ago was that?" I asked.

"Long enough," she answered. "I've been here a long time."

"So what did you do?"

"I met some people who introduced me to some other people who taught me how to shoplift. I did that for a while with them until one of them got caught. Then I got a job waiting tables. I did that for a while, then got my GED. I thought about going to college, but I never did."

"Why not?" I asked.

"That plan changed when I got knocked up for the first time." She chuckled. "The daddy was the Mexican busboy who worked where I worked. We only did it once. After that, he got sent back to Mexico. I never saw him again."

"Did you love him?"

"Love him? No. I scarcely knew him. That time, though, I got lucky. A piece of liver dropped out of me one day, and it was over. Just like that. Gone. It was probably waiting tables that did it. All that walking. I was working really long hours back then.

"I stayed at that job for another year. Then I met Mooch.

"Mooch was a brother, and he was older than me by about fifteen years. I *loved* that man. He was like the father that Odell never was. And he loved me, he loved me as a person. He would talk to me when I was depressed, maybe even buy me a little gift. You know, earrings or a trip to Red Lobster. He was the first real friend I ever had. He's the one who trained me, showed me how to use the stuff I got."

She gave me what I suspect she thought was a knowing look. She raised her eyebrows and lowered them slowly as she looked me straight in the eye. I pretended not to notice.

"The first time we did it," she continued, "*I* had to ask *him*. He treated me like a little girl, and I wanted to show him I was a woman. And you know what he did? He asked me if I was sure. I wasn't a virgin, and I told him so. I figured my time with Odell had prepared me to satisfy any man. Boy, was I wrong! Mooch rode me like a horse! I used to feel sorry for Abbey, because Odell was fucking me. After Mooch, I felt sorry for Abbey because all she would ever know was Odell. Mooch rode me so hard, I had bruises on the insides of my thighs. By the time he was through, we both had sweat rolling off of us. It was wonderful.

"Two weeks later, he told me I was ready. He wanted me to quit waiting tables, and move in with him and the two other women he lived with. He had told me about them, but I was still scared when he introduced me. To my surprise, they were glad to have me there. Gladys, his bottom woman, looked at me and said, 'Yeah. Now we gon' make some serious money.' I didn't know how the game worked, but Gladys told me not to worry, they would take care of everything.

She was almost like the mother Abbey had never been. And I didn't remember my real mother anymore. We truly were like family."

She went on to explain that Mooch's clientele changed after she arrived. He got lawyers and accountants downtown who were willing to pay well for her services. Gladys had been right. They did well. At least for a little while. Then things began to go bad.

"Missy, the other girl who lived with us," Bev went on, "had met a boy somewhere, and thought she was in love. She made the mistake of telling them she wanted to get out of the life. Mooch and Gladys both kicked her ass so bad, she was in the hospital for a month. She had been a cute girl, too. Dark skin like polished wood, and a short 'fro. Beautiful tits. The kind with the nipples that stick way out. Men used to love her tits, because when they sucked them, she would go wild. We were the professionals. We were the ones that were supposed to stay in control. But Missy couldn't help it. She always lost control when someone with a nice tongue began to work on her.

"I remember once we did a threesome for a client Mooch had just gotten. Missy and me and this little skinny-assed Oreo judge in some hotel not far off State Street. He'd never done a threesome before, and this was his dream-come-true. So we worked him. He'd fuck me and eat her, then fuck her and eat me. Each time about thirty seconds before he'd want to change. He was in his little world, and everything looked like it was under control. This was going to be some easy money.

"That's when he started sucking Missy's tits. I knew we were in trouble when she moaned. I could see her letting those big, brown cow eyes of hers roll up into her head. She rolled over onto that little man, and stuffed her whole left tit into his mouth. The man was terrified.

She stuffed his dick inside her, and he came in about ten seconds. Now he was embarrassed. All he wanted to do was get out, but he wasn't strong enough to get her off him. He looked over at me with such sad eyes." She chuckled remembering him. "So I crawled into bed next to him, and began sucking on her other tit. She knew that I knew how to work her tits the way she liked it. We had done this before. She crawled off him and onto me. She sucked my tits while I sucked hers for about an hour, but it only took the judge about five minutes to get dressed and run."

She paused for a moment. Now her voice got sad. "To this day," she said, "I've never understood why, but after kicking her ass until she was bleeding from her nose and bruises around both eyes and from a gash in her scalp, Gladys cut her. Right across her cheek." She gestured with her finger across her own cheek. "And Mooch let her do it. It wasn't a bad cut. In fact, it healed up so good, it hardly left a scar. But it changed her. The boy she had wanted to marry left her when he found out what she did for a living. I think that hurt her more than the ass kicking and the cut. She became cold as ice.

"Not long after Missy got out of the hospital, I got knocked up again. Mooch was the daddy, and Gladys was pissed. I didn't know this at the time, but Mooch wasn't supposed to be still fucking me. He was supposed to be just fucking Gladys. My pussy was supposed to be strictly for making money. Gladys demanded that I get an abortion, but Mooch said no. This was so Abbey and Odell. I couldn't believe that I was in that exact same situation again. Gladys attacked me for sleeping with-- as she put it-- her nigger. She started trying to kick me in the stomach. I ran for the door, and into the middle of the street. Gladys followed me. She hit me a couple of times. But before she could really do anything, a cop car pulled up. That's when I met Avel. He jumped out, kicked Gladys's ass, then arrested her. He arrested Mooch, too, but he let me go." She paused for a long moment. "Yup," she continued, "my life was about to be fucked up for real, because the last thing I needed at that time was a baby, and no family to help me raise it."

All of a sudden, she was out of her storytelling reverie. Anything else I learned about Avel, I would have to learn from him. She was matter-of-fact about what had to be done. "His partner's name is Macklin," she said. "We can use him to get what we need."

XIII

It was three months before Mama took me back to Miss Blue's house. I couldn't help myself. I brushed by her, and made a beeline for the kitchen hoping to see Miss Abbey.

"You must really want some cookies and milk," Miss Blue said, misinterpreting my headlong rush.

"Yes," I said. My voice sounded deflated when I saw Miss Abbey wasn't there.

Miss Blue ushered me to my usual seat, and I sat down. She moved about the kitchen getting dishes, warming and pouring milk, selecting cookies, and all the while, I watched her from the corner of my eye. I wondered how similar she was to Miss Abbey under her dress. When she sat down, I had to force myself not to stare at her lap, and search for her scent with each breath that I drew. Instead, all I could smell was her sweat. It was not the same.

"Sue came by the other day," she said. "She asked about you."

I bit into a cookie.

"She's my best friend and all, but she is a strange duck," Miss Blue said.

I wanted to blurt out that I knew, and that she had let me see between her legs. But then I remembered that I had crossed my heart and hoped to die. I took a sip of milk, swished it around with the chewed up cookie, and swallowed.

"She's the real reason Sydney and me had to leave Arkansas."

I looked at her, then sipped some more milk.

"When we were young, we did everything together. We were as close as sisters. The only thing we saw differently was Sydney."

"I don't understand," I said.

"Somebody started the rumor that Sydney killed a man in Florida with his bare hands. Strangled him to death."

"Did he?" I asked.

"Of course not! Back then, Sydney was as gentle as a summer breeze. That's why I loved him. He was big and gorgeous and sweet."

I stuffed the rest of the first cookie into my mouth.

"Sue's problem was that she was jealous. She had never had a man of her own, and she wanted mine. She never said it, but I knew that she wanted to tell my daddy about Sydney and me. So we left. We ran away together. The problem was that men didn't like her. My daddy didn't like her, and Sydney *still* doesn't like her." She shook her head. "Poor thing. Poor, poor thing."

"Why don't men like her?" I asked. I found it hard to imagine that anyone wouldn't like a person with that wonderful smell.

"She was a prude," she said. "She still is. She won't let a man . . ." She hesitated wondering how much to say.

". . . put his thing in her?" I finished the sentence for her, then I regretted it. I was instantly afraid that I had said too much.

"Yes," she said, "put his thing in her."

My fear surged in the pause she left after her last utterance. I was certain that she was about to confront me with how I knew about the things men and women do.

"I'll bet that she has never even once been touched by another person," she harrumphed.

I quickly sipped some milk and swallowed.

She sighed. "I will have to give her this, though," she said, "she has been a staunch friend. She saved my life once when we were back home, and since being here, she has been like a rock."

"Maybe she loves you," I said.

"She does," she answered. "We're still just like sisters."

I bit into another cookie.

"And when Sydney began to change," she continued, "she was always there for me."

"You should live together," I said, talking around my food.

She chuckled. "We couldn't do that. I'm married. Besides, . . ." Her voice trailed off.

"She's a prude?" I ventured. I reached for my glass.

"Yes," she answered firmly, "she is too much the prude."

I wanted to drink some milk before the words I felt forming in my mouth could escape, but I was too slow. "Maybe she's not the prude you think she is," I said.

Miss Blue snapped her head in my direction, and stared at me. I stared into my glass as I poured milk too quickly into my mouth. I gagged, and spit milk down my front and into the saucer onto my last cookie.

"Are you alright?" Miss Blue hopped up and began patting me hard on the back.

I couldn't catch my breath. My heart was pounding. I was afraid it was going to stop.

Miss Blue grabbed a dishrag, and cleaned me up after I was finally able to breathe again. She cleaned up the table and wiped my chair. "I think you've had enough," she said.

"I'm sorry," I said. I sat back down.

"Don't be sorry," she said. "Mistakes do happen."

I knew she meant to say 'accidents do happen,' but her mind wasn't on what she was saying. I could tell that she was consumed with making a mental tally of all the mistakes she had made in her life. With each passing moment, she seemed to sink deeper and deeper into her melancholy. Then, almost out of the blue, she said, "Maybe we *could* live together." She was silent for another long moment. Then she said, "Sydney's never here anyway. He wouldn't even miss me."

"Did you ask Miss Abbey?" I asked.

"Ask her what?"

"If you could live with her."

"No," she said. There was a tone of doubt in her voice as if she had not considered the option that Miss Abbey might say no. Finally, she said, "But I don't think she would mind." Miss Blue smiled and touched my hand, "I think you've come up with a good idea."

I felt good inside. I was a child, and I had helped a grown-up. I felt big.

XIV

Bev's plan had worked like a charm. Macklin delivered him up at the appointed time, noon on a Monday, at the garage behind Bev's apartment building. We stuffed him into the trunk of my car, and Bev and I drove him back to the garage behind what used to be my building on the south side. Bev helped me get him out of the trunk and onto a chair that I had set up. I tied him down and put a hood over his head. I had him exactly where I wanted him. I told Bev to watch from a corner, and keep quiet. When he came to, I started asking him questions.

"What's your name?" I asked.

"Where am I? Where's Macklin?" He wanted to rub his face, but his hands were tied behind his back. He felt what he thought was an ice cube under his shirt.

"What's your name?" I asked again.

"I'm not telling you shit," Avel said, "'til you tell me what this is all about. Why am I blindfolded? Why am I tied to this chair?"

"These are just precautions," I answered.

"Against what?"

"You trying to leave too soon." I paused a moment. "Tell us your name."

"Avel," he said.

"What do you do?"

"I'm a cop," he said, "and I'm the one who should be asking the fucking questions."

"You don't ask the questions here, Avel."

"Where is here? And who the fuck are you?"

"How long have you been a cop?"

"How did I get here, anyway?"

"How long have you been a cop?"

"The last thing I remember, we were doing a stakeout."

"How long have you been a cop?" I asked again.

"It was the coffee, wasn't it? There was something in the fucking coffee."

"How long have you been a cop?"

"Twenty years," Avel said. "I've been a cop for twenty years."

"Why did you become a cop?"

"I remember, now. It *was* the coffee! We were staking out this house. We thought it might be a crack house."

"Were you going to bust it?" I asked.

"No, we were . . . Who are you? What is this about?"

"Were you going to bust it?"

"I smell gun oil. Are there weapons in here?"

"Were you going to bust it?"

"No."

"Then why were you staking it out?"

"I became a cop because I wanted to make a difference," he said.

Then he had a strange remembrance. Maybe his life was beginning to flash before his eyes. The road ahead was dark. His father looked from the road ahead to the dashboard then back to the road. His father was driving too carefully, almost as if he didn't want to rock the car too much.

The engine sputtered, and he heard his father catch his breath. It smoothed out, and his father relaxed a little. His father studied the dashboard again, shifting his head to change the angle of the needle on the hash marks. The engine sputtered again, and his father farted. It smoothed out again, but he didn't really relax this time. He gripped the wheel waiting for something else to happen.

The engine stopped.

"Goddamn it!" his father said, slamming his hand into the wheel.

"It's okay, daddy," he said.

His father took a deep breath. "We have to walk," his father said.

"I can walk," he said.

"Yeah, but this is niggerville, and we ain't niggers."

"Have you made the kind of difference you wanted to make?" I asked.

Avel paused. "No."

"Why is that?"

"I got sidetracked."

"Meaning?"

"It's tough out there in the streets."

"And?"

"And sometimes it's hard to change things."

"Did you try?"

"Yes!" He paused. "At first, I did."

"What happened?"

"Things changed."

"Things?"

"*I* changed," he said.

"How did you change?"

"What is this?" he asked.

"It's an investigation."

"Well, who's being investigated?"

"You are," I answered.

"Me?! What am I being investigated for?"

"Never mind that for now."

"Where's my lawyer?"

"You won't have a lawyer here. In this investigation, you have to speak for yourself."

"I demand a lawyer! Who's the investigator?! Are you guys feds? I'm a detective, too. All of the feds like me. We work good together. I stay out of their way."

"We are the investigators."

"Well, who the fuck are 'we?'"

"We'll get to that later, too. Right now, we want to know why you didn't make a difference."

"What's niggerville, daddy?"

"Niggerville is where niggers live."

"Who are niggers?"

"Niggers are 'coons, jungle bunnies, darkies, jig-a-boos. You know, black folks."

"Is my friend, Andy, a nigger?"

"Yeah, he's a nigger."

"Why is he a nigger."

"Because his mommy and daddy are niggers."

"I like Andy."

"No, you don't. You don't like niggers 'cause I don't like niggers. And I want you should stop playing with him."

"But I like Andy. I like niggers."

His father grabbed him and slapped him hard in the mouth.

"Don't you ever fuckin' say that again. You hear me? Niggers are dirty and dumb. They stink. And you stay away from them."

"The question is, why didn't you make a difference?" I asked.

"I already told you," he said. "I got sidetracked."

"How did you get sidetracked?"

"I got stuck with a partner who didn't care."

"Meaning?"

"Meaning he didn't care. He was a veteran of twenty years, and he told me there is no justice in the streets."

"And you believed him?"

"I didn't at first."

"But?"

"But I began to realize little by little that he was right. I wanted to catch the big fish, but he told me the big fish were too big. They were too politically connected. I wanted to catch the medium fish, but they had too much money at their disposal. They could pay bail, jump to Mexico or Columbia. Fly back to Moscow. It was part of the cost of doing business. That left only the little fish, the wannabes. But getting one of them is like getting a roach. There's a million more where that one came from."

"So you gave up?"

"I like to think I became more prudent."

"When did you begin taking the money?"

"That's it!" he said. "Get me the fuck out of here." He lurched in the chair trying to break free.

"When did you begin taking the money?"

"Fuck you! I never took no money!"

His father got out of the car, and went around to the trunk to get the gas can. A car pulled up behind theirs. "Y'all need some help?" a voice called out.

"Naw," his father answered, "I got it."

"You sure?"

"I'm sure."

As the car pulled off, another voice from the car blurted out, "What's a honky doing over in this 'hood?"

The car was snow white with a continental kit and fender skirts in the back. The rear of the car was weighted lower than the front. The hood ornament was a galloping horse.

Suddenly, it stopped, the brake lights glowing a bright red. He could tell that the men in the car were arguing. The car bounced a couple of the times as the brakes were applied and released. Then the brake lights went off and the car sped away.

"That was close," his father said. There was a noticeable quaver in his voice. His father was standing by the side of the car with the gas can in hand. His father motioned him out of the car. The two of them began walking in the direction away from the white car.

His father and he walked about half a block before he heard the roar of an engine behind them. He could feel his father's hand squeeze his. He looked over his shoulder. A set of headlights bore down on the two of them. The lights swerved at the last moment and the snow white car screeched to a stop beside them.

"You a long way from home, ain't you, honky?"

There was a long pause.

"What's a honky, daddy?"

There was another pause.

"Tell him what a honky is, honky."

"White people," his father said.

"Tell him that you a honky."

"I'm a honky."

"Tell him that he's a honky."

"You're a honky, son."

"Are they niggers, daddy?"

"Where's my partner?" he asked. "Where's Macklin?"

"Let's cut to the chase, shall we?"

"Meaning what?"

"I know why you were staking out that house."

"Okay, smart guy," he said, "why?"

"You were staking out that house so you could figure out how much money they made."

"Why did we need to know that?"

"You wanted to take a cut."

"Did Macklin tell you that?"

"Never mind how we know," I said. "Just tell me how big a cut?"

Avel paused, then said, "Thirty percent."

"That's a lot."

"That's what I told him."

"And?"

"He said we had to get that much if I wanted to get a piece of the action, too."

"And you said?"

"I didn't say anything."

"So you took the money?"

"I never got a chance to. Mack gave me a cup of coffee that he had picked up before coming to work."

His father's whole body jerked.

"Say what, li'l bro'?" A shadowy face in the front seat leaned forward. "What did you say?"

Nobody answered. There was a loud click from the back seat. His father began to tremble, like he recognized that sound. The sound was like a padlock being snapped closed. He pulled Avel behind his leg, but Avel wanted to see what was happening. He stuck his head around. There was a flash of blue light that lit up the entire inside of the car, and the thunderous sound of a shot. He could see the silhouette of three men in the car, two in front, one in back. His father dropped to his knees, then dropped Avel's hand. He rolled over onto his shoulder. The smell of smoke stung the inside of Avel's face. It stung his throat. It burned the inside of his chest. He knew what had happened, but he hoped he was wrong. He hoped that if he didn't move, maybe it would be okay. Maybe his daddy wouldn't die. Maybe. He stood as still as he could. He didn't even breathe.

The snow white car with the horse on the hood pulled away.

"Did Mack slip me a Mickey?"

"Were you a virgin?"

"Yes."

"In twenty years, you never took a bribe?"

"No."

"Did you take any money at all?"

"Well, yeah," he said, "but it wasn't a bribe."

"What was it?"

"It was a gift. It was a token of appreciation."

"How big were these tokens?"

"Some of them were big."

"How big?"

"A couple hundred."

"And what were these people appreciative of?"

"As a rule, they were glad I didn't kick their ass."

"How often did you refrain from kicking somebody's ass?"

"Once, maybe twice a week."

Avel stood still not breathing for a long minute. Then his father groaned, "Avel, son, help me."

He scrambled to the ground, and turned his father's head so his face won't be in the dirt. "Daddy," he sobbed. "Don't die, daddy." He didn't want to cry, but the tears came up by themselves. He tried to sniff them away, but they spilled down his cheeks and splashed onto his father's face, mixing with the dirt and the blood and the spit from his mouth.

"Remember that car, son," his father said. "Remember that car and this number: . . ." His father gave him the license number.

"Don't die, daddy," he said, trying to hold his father's head level when it began to grow heavy in his hands and wanted to roll off his lap. "Please, don't die."

The police came with blue lights flashing and screeching tires and tender words. "It's okay, son," one of them said. "We'll get you home."

"Will my daddy be okay?" he asked.

"What's your address?" the officer asked back.

He told them what he could, but he couldn't remember it all. He couldn't remember the number. He told them it was a white car. The officer relayed the message on his radio as a ". . . light-colored sedan."

A week later, they took him and his mother down to the station. "We caught them," they said. "This is the car." It wasn't the same one.

It had no skirts, no continental kit. "We're going to show you a line-up." They took him into a small room with a large window. There were four men sitting in a row in chairs. "Are these the men who shot your father?"

"Tell them yes," his mother said, choking back tears.

"I think so," he answered.

"Are you sure?"

"It's the wrong car," he said.

"We found a gun in that car."

"It's the wrong color."

"It's the same caliber," they said.

The police seemed to understand his mother's pain. They understood his loss. They smiled at him, and rubbed his head just like his father did. They even talked like his father. They called him son.

"Who did you take these tokens from?" I asked.

"Folks in my district."

"Black folks, white folks?"

"Niggers mostly."

"You don't like niggers, do you?"

"I don't dislike niggers. I don't like niggers. They're just a nuisance is all." He shifted in his seat. "Look, I'm a cop. I'm a good cop. I know what I'm doing, and I ain't scared to do it."

"Did Macklin take the money?"

"I guess so."

"You guess?"

"He took the money," he said. "Are you guys with OPS?"

"No."

"Then who are you?"

"We are the people."

"You must be a prosecutor."

"What makes you think that?"

"Prosecutors do that all the time."

"Do what?"

"Tell a suspect that he represents the people knowing these clowns will think that he represents them."

"Why would he do that?"

"To gain their confidence so they'll confess."

"Do *you* want to confess?"

"To what?"

"Anything."

"Hell, no."

"It would go easier if you did."

"I know this technique, asshole," he said. "I've used it myself."

"What technique?"

"The technique of getting an innocent person to confess."

"Why would you do that?"

"Do what?"

"Make an innocent man confess."

"To close the case."

"What about getting the right man?"

"If he confesses, he *is* the right man."

"Even if he is innocent?"

"There is no justice in the streets."

"What about in the courts?"

"Court justice is an extension of street justice."

"In other words, no justice?"

"No justice."

"What do you see your job as?"

"A street cleaner," he answered.

"Explain that."

"There are folks on the street who shouldn't be there," he said. "I clean them up."

"Who determines who shouldn't be there?"

"I do."

"Suppose they didn't do anything?"

"I'll make something up."

"Give me an example."

"Listen," he said, "I've given you what you wanted. Now give me something."

"What do you want?" I asked back.

"I want to know who you are."

"Your chances of survival are inversely proportional to the amount you know about me."

"Meaning what?"

"I could tell you, but then I'd have to kill you."

"So," he said, "are you a Hell's Angel?"

I didn't answer.

"What about a Gangster Disciple?"

Still no response.

"Not an angel, not a disciple. What about an apostle?"

"Fine," I answered.

"Now which one? Peter? Paul? John? What's your name?"

"Whatever."

"Oh, I get it. You're the thirteenth apostle."

"Cool."

"Who do you serve?"

"Huh?"

"I'm the good guy here, serving God. Who do *you* serve?"

"Did God tell you to knock off that crack house?"

"Thirteen is an unlucky number. Besides, Jesus only had twelve apostles. The thirteenth apostle must be an evil apostle."

"I do what I want."

"Everybody serves somebody."

"I already told you," I answered, "I serve the people."

"Well, how about that? So do I. Are we on the same team?"

"Not even! That you serve them is a fiction; that I serve them is a fact."

"How does bringing me here serve the people?"

"You're a thug. You were supposed to close that crack house. Instead, you elected to get a part of the action."

"I had to," he said.

"Oh?" I asked.

"It's part of the code."

"In that?"

"Everybody in the station knows about that house," he said. "That's why no squads ever cruise by it."

"Was everybody in the station on the take?" I asked.

"No," he answered, "not everybody. But everybody knew who was, and everybody avoided breaking it up."

"There was a story on the news a while back about a young man who hanged himself while in police custody," I said. "Wasn't that at your district?"

I knew he could feel his temperature rising.

"Is that what this is about?" he asked.

"Was it at you district?" I asked again.

"Yes."

"What was the kid's name?"

"They called him Duc, short for Ducats," he answered. "His real name was Marcus Pemberly."

"That's right," I said. "And how old was Duc?"

"Seventeen."

"And whose case was he?" I asked.

"He was mine," Avel answered. "Mine and Macklin's."

Then I said, "You've got a daughter, don't you?"

"How did you know that?"

"We know a lot about you," I said.

I could tell he was beginning to panic. This time he yelled, "How did you know that?"

"Her name is Jessica," I said to him. "She's fourteen, and she's pregnant."

"She was raped," he said.

"I know," I told him.

XV

That's when he told me about her.

He was depositing money at an ATM. He signed his name, Avel something, on the back of the check, and slipped it into the envelope. Did he tell me his last name? Maybe he didn't have one. He was just Avel. Avel was as Avel did. If I had to guess, I would have guessed that his last name was Mann. Avel Mann. But that would only have been a guess. There were parts of his story that he never got around to telling me. I mean, it's not like we were close or anything like that.

He gathered just the right amount of moisture on his tongue, and licked the flap. One clean stroke. No wasted moves. It's a chore he had done a hundred times, and he did it with mechanical precision using a minimum of movements. His fingers were already in position to press the flap down, again in one clean stroke. For Avel, everything in life was like an assembly line. The right move at the right time at the right angle. Nothing more; nothing less. He was like Data from Star Trek.

"Dad," Jessica had said to him, "you are such a nerd! Look at you! You move like a robot."

He was dismissive. After all, what did *she* know? She was thirteen. She had zits and braces. He lowered the driver-side window. He slipped the bank card from his pocket, and slid it directly into the slot of the ATM. He punched in the code: 1248. Fast cash: $60.00. He took the receipt. He took the card. He scooted them each into their respective places in the wallet, then put the wallet away. He started the car, shifted into gear, and drove off.

"We're going the wrong way!" she said. "You're going to make me late!"

"You'll be fine," he told her.

"It's over on Sheridan Road, by the lake."

"Yes, I know."

"We're not by the lake, dad!"

"We're five minutes from it."

"We're a long way from it, dad," she said, "heading in the wrong direction!"

He took a left at Broadway, then a right onto Thorndale. A couple of stop signs, and he was at Sheridan Road. The lake was dead ahead. He didn't say anything. He turned left and cruised to Berger Park.

"Here we are," he said. He cut his eye to the clock on the dash. "Fourteen fifty-five. We're early."

She was at that awkward stage. Her legs were getting longer, but she still had those big puppy feet. She was growing buds on her chest. She was nonplused. She grabbed at the door handle, but in her haste to swing the door open and get out, her hand slipped off. The handle thumped back into place. She gripped the handle firmly, and yanked while throwing her shoulder into the door.

"You have to unlock it first," he told her.

Still holding the handle, she trust her thumb at the doorlock. She bent the nail back, and yelped in pain.

"Can I help you?" he offered.

"No-wah!" She sniffed back tears. She was desperate not to cry in front of him.

Saying no with two syllables meant she was embarrassed but wanted to make it look as if she were mad. To her, anger was a more acceptable emotion to exhibit than embarrassment. She finally got the door open and stumbled out. She concealed her thumb in a curled fist.

"I love you," he said. "I'll pick you up at eighteen hundred hours."
She slammed the door.

He watched her as she walked towards the building. She was beginning to walk like her mother used to walk, with that little pinched-butt switch, almost as if her knees were latched together with a short chain.

Bev had been a good wife, and he missed her. He missed the meatloaf made with canned soup. The spaghetti with too much bite. The cling peaches and Maraschino cherries. He began to feel that softness in his heart, but then he blocked it out. She was dead. She had been dead for ten years. In his mind, at least, if not in reality. In fact, fuck her! She wasn't a good wife, she was a bitch. How could she run off like that? After all he had done for her. She was already knocked up when he met her. He saved her. She was on the street, and her black-assed pimp was kicking her ass. He could have run her in, but he didn't. He kicked the pimp's ass, and ran him in, instead. He came back for her. He bought her a meal. He put her up at his place for the night. He cleaned her up. He got her a job, taught her how to get up every morning and go to work. It wasn't much, temping at an ad agency, but at least she had some honest money coming in. And she seemed to be taking to it. She would have gotten promoted, but by then, the baby was almost due.

After Jessica was born, Bev stayed home to take care of her. Those first few weeks were tough. Jessica was up at all hours of the day and night, and Bev was constantly up feeding her. Sometimes, he would get up and walk with her to make her burp. He hadn't even screwed Bev yet, and he was playing daddy to her newborn child.

Bev was the one who brought up the six-week waiting period. He was content to just be helping someone clean up their life. Five weeks went by, and Bev mentioned, almost in passing, that she could hardly wait this last week. Then on the fifth day of the last week, she came into the living room where he had decided to sleep since she began staying with him. He was on the couch under a blanket. She slipped under it with him.

"Where's the baby?" he asked.

"The baby is fine," she said.

She nestled her face into his neck, and slid one leg over his, her cottony tits on his chest. He wasn't quite sure what to do, but his dick got hard as a rock. She stroked it a couple of times, then put it inside her. He could scarcely feel the sides. It didn't have a bottom. She sat up straddling his body as if she were riding a horse. She rocked her pelvis in a riding motion. He wanted to match her rocking, but when he did, it broke her cadence. He couldn't do it in sync. "Just lie still," she said. He did. She raised herself up enough that he slipped out of her, then she sat back down guiding his dick into her ass. It was nice and tight, and a moan escaped from his mouth. This was the way her pussy was supposed to feel. She horse-rocked again as she fondled her pussy. He came first, then she came. She rested forward on his chest again. He reached his hand around to feel her butt. She arched her back so he could feel his come oozing from her ass.

"I love you," she said.

"Marry me," he said back.

"Yes," she said.

There was something in her voice that sounded as if she had just scored a victory.

"Yes," she said again. "Yes."

Though it was another six months before he actually got around to making it down to City Hall, she slipped easily into the wife role immediately. When she first got there, she ate what he ate, cereal and cheap TV dinners. Now that they were engaged, she cooked. For breakfast, he had toaster waffles, brown-and-serve sausages, and little plastic bottles of orange drink. He still ate a lot of TV dinners, but they were the expensive kind. On special occasions, she went all out. She boiled spaghetti, warmed a jar of sauce, the good kind, and warmed some frozen French bread. She also liked trying those soup can recipes for meatloaf, dips and gravy. Life was good.

It lasted about three years. It started with Bev getting to be stand-offish. He didn't worry too much about it, though. She was like that sometimes. Then there were the phone calls. She would answer the phone sometimes, and her demeanor would change. Her conversations seemed disjointed, as if the words she spoke had a secondary meaning that was disclosed only in the tone or timbre of her voice. Once, only once, he answered the phone, and the caller hanged up. Finally, there was the mouse under her left eye. She swore it was from falling face first on the kitchen table, but her description was too full, too detailed.

Then he caught them. It was luck, sheer luck. He picked up the phone to make a call at exactly the same moment Bev had picked it up. But she was quicker than he was. She took pride in having fast fingers. This time, it gave her away. While he was still contemplating the numbers he wanted to dial, she had her numbers punched. He wondered who she could be calling, but he didn't say anything. He covered the receiver to conceal his breathing. A man answered. A brother.

"Yo," the brother said instead of "hello."

Bev said, "hi." Then she caught her breath like she did sometimes when she got excited.

"Baby girl," he said, his low-toned voice slipping into an effortless silkiness. "I'm really sorry about . . ."

"Who the fuck is this?" Avel blurted out.

Whoever it was slammed the phone down.

Bev had screamed, "What are you . . . I mean . . . I mean . . ."

"Who the fuck is this?" he blurted into the phone again.

Then he could hear her clumping down the hall from the bedroom to the living room. She sounded like a goddamn cow. Clump, clump, clump.

"Baby," she said, "I'm sorry. I'm sorry."

"Who was that?"

"Um . . . Um . . . That was my parole officer."

"Parole officer?! Why are you calling him?"

"I have to."

"Why? You're not on parole."

"Not now, but I was."

"So why are you calling him now?"

"I just wanted to make sure there wasn't no last little something I had to do."

"Like what?"

"I don't know, honey," she said. "I just don't want anything to come up and break us up. I love you so much." She got down on her knees and pulled his dick out and sucked it.

"But . . . But . . .," he said.

She put his dick so far in her mouth, his nuts bumped her chin. "Oh, my god!" His knees began to quiver, then his whole body. He came. She swallowed. Less than a minute later, he came again. His knees were so weak, he dropped onto the couch. He tried to open his eyes, but he couldn't. He was out cold, and he knew it.

It was the baby crying that woke him up. Still weak, he got up and went to the bedroom. The baby was sitting up in bed crying. She had had a bad dream. He got her a glass of water from the bathroom, and gave it to her. She took two swallows, then gave it back. She dove back into her pillow. He waddled out to the kitchen, and sat down at the kitchen table. There was a yellow post-it stuck to the sugar bowl. It read: 'It's been fun. Bev.'

Well, it had been fun, Bev. Too bad you missed it. Jessica was a wonderful young woman.

He watched as Jessica approached the steps to the mansion in Berger Park. She stumbled on the first step, then caught herself. He could tell that she wanted to look around to see if he saw her stumble. She was strong. She didn't look. She opened the door with poise, and stepped inside. He put the car into gear, and eased away from the curb.

He drove to the station over on Clark Street, and changed into his work clothes. It was his partner's turn to drive, and just as well. He was preoccupied with Jessica. Maybe he should have attended to that thumb. His partner, Macklin, a ruddy-faced man with close-cropped white hair mumbled something about picking someone up. They talked, but his mind was on not being late picking Jessica up. He was proud of himself. Not many men would raise a child that wasn't his own for ten years.

"You know the place," Macklin said. "It's over on Lunt just off Sheridan."

"What?"

"The house where we're making the pickup."

"What house?"

"Forget about it," Macklin said. "I'll take care of it."

Macklin drove the grey sedan east on Morse, then cut north up the alley to Lunt. He stopped the car before actually reaching the street.

"That's the place," Macklin said pointing to one of the apartment buildings across the street.

"Which one?" Avel asked.

"Wait here," Macklin said. He opened the driver's side door, and hopped out. Macklin loped across Lunt and continued up the alley. Half way up the length of that stretch of the alley, another part of the alley met it to form a T. Macklin turned left, and disappeared from view.

Avel waited about 30 seconds wondering what the hell Macklin could have been doing. He took a couple of big gulps of coffee. Then he heard a pop. It was a gun shot from the area where Macklin had turned in the alley.

Avel slung open the door. Stepping out, he felt excited. He heard two more shots. He pulled his service pistol and thought about Jessica. He was about to make the world a safer place. He ran across Lunt and up the alley following the way Macklin had gone. He rounded the corner, and stopped. The alley was clear, but he could smell gun smoke. His vision blurred for a moment as his pulse throbbed in his temples. He drew in a deep breath. He eased closer to the garage door on his far right. His legs began to feel rubbery. His weapon felt heavy in his hand. Its weight pulled his arm toward the pavement. He needed to sit down. He wanted to take a shit, but this was neither the place nor the time. It was time to get tough.

"Avel!" It was Macklin's voice. "Avel, I'm around here."

He stepped forward towards the gangway next to the garage. He peeked around the corner, then jerked his head back.

"It's safe," Macklin said. "It's over."

Macklin had his pistol drawn; the kid stood right in front of Macklin with his hands folded behind his head. Avel recognized the kid from a couple of days earlier. He remembered picking the kid up. It had been his own idea. The kid had been standing on the corner of Glenwood and Granville, in front of the liquor store. The kid had worn a fire engine red warmup and baggy red pants hanging so low on his ass, they were on the verge of falling around his ankles. It was the same outfit he was wearing now, bleeding. The kid's boxer shorts were the same bright red.

Macklin and he had been parked on Granville heading west just on the east side of Glenwood. The kid bopped around the corner in their direction. He was dancing to something he was listening to on his headsets.

"That little nigger's time is running out," Avel had said.

"Why," Macklin asked. "What'd he do?"

"He pissed me off. That little nigger pissed me the fuck off."

"What'd he do?" Macklin asked again.

"He smirked."

"Huh?"

"He smirked *at me.*"

"So what are we going to do?"

Avel had dropped the car into drive and turned on the blue lights. He gunned the engine; the car leaped into traffic. "Follow my lead," he had said. He squealed the car through the intersection and screeched to a stop on the wrong side of the street.

They jumped out of the car. Avel grabbed the kid and slammed him against the car. He whipped out his piece, and pointed it right in the kid's face.

"What's up with that?" the kid asked, his hands in the air shaking.

"Smirk now, nigger," Avel said.

"I ain't smirking! I ain't smirking!"

"I'm taking your black ass down for the last time you smirked." Avel was pissed.

"That wasn't none o' me."

"It damn sure wasn't your Aunt Ja-Mammy."

Just then, the kid knocked the gun away and sprinted back around the corner. Avel was caught completely off guard. The gun skidded a good twenty feet away. Avel looked like a character out of one of those old silent movies, starting left, stopping, starting right, stopping, looking around at the ground like a crazy man, then finally spotting the gun and lunging for it like a salmon lunging for a worm. The kid really made him look bad. "I'm killing him," Avel had said. "I'm killing him if it's the last thing I do."

"What's going on?" Avel asked while still pressing his back against the garage door.

Macklin said, "We need to . . ."

Just then, Avel wheeled around the corner of the garage, and fired at the kid hitting him in the temple. The kid dropped like a sand bag. A pencil-thin stream of blood arced from his head. "It was self defense," Avel said. "He swung at me with a stick." Avel surveyed the ground immediately around the kid's body. Finding a popsicle stick, he dragged it with his foot to within reach of the kid's hand. "There," he said, "it was self defense."

"For Christ sake, Avel," Macklin said, "it's a popsicle stick!"

"He was good with weapons," Avel said. "Besides, as long as you keep your mouth shut, no one will know."

"You shot him in cold blood."

"I should have made him suck my dick first? So it could have been in warm blood?"

Macklin shifted his weight from one side to the other. "I wanted to make it right about the other day. I got him so you wouldn't have to shoot him."

"Okay," Avel said. "Now it's right. And thanks. You made it easy for me."

"I can't keep covering for you like this," Macklin said.

"But now you can't *stop* covering for me," Avel answered back. "You've covered enough shit that now you're an accessory. If I go down, you go down."

"But why did you have to shot him?"

"What was I going to do, kick his ass?"

"Yes," Macklin answered, "kick his ass! What's wrong with kicking his ass instead of killing him?"

"Yesterday, that might have worked," Avel said. "But today, I needed to kill somebody."

"What does that mean?" Macklin was getting mad. "You *needed* to *kill* somebody?"

"Everybody's got needs. You got needs. I got needs."

"Yeah, but my needs don't include snuffing somebody's lights out."

"So now you're better than me?" Avel was getting mad, too.

"No, but leaving a string of dead bodies lying around presents a problem every now and then."

"The only problem is that you don't want to keep your mouth shut any more."

"I can't," Macklin said, "I just can't."

"Why not?" Avel asked. "I've killed a dozen of these punks, and they all deserved it. Why the sudden problem now?"

"It's not sudden," Macklin said. "I've hated it all along."

"Well, that's just tough shit. Like I said, if I go down, you're coming with me."

Avel relaxed. Realizing he had told me way more than he had initially intended, he said, "It didn't take much to get him to co-operate with you, did it?"

"So after killing that kid, you picked up your own kid and took her home."

"Yeah," he said, " it was easy. Killing him made my kid safer."

"No," I said. "He didn't turn on you until we offered him the money. But it didn't take much."

I could tell that he was thinking this was about to get messy. He felt along the back edge of the seat of his chair. There was a nick in the metal, a nick with a sharp point at the corner.

He began to fidget in his seat as a cover for rubbing the cords on his wrists across the nick. He needed to distract me. "Hey, man," he said, "I've got to take a piss." He felt that rubbing the cord over the nick was working. The cords felt loose on his wrists. "Aw, man, please! Don't let me piss in my pants."

It was probably a bad idea, but I let him think his ruse was working. I wanted to fuck with his head. I turned my back on him. He worked the cords loose, and snatched the blindfold off. Bev didn't know what

I was doing, so she shouted, "Oh!" I spun back around with my nine millimeter out, cocked, and pointed at his face.

"What are *you* doing here?" he asked Bev. Until now, he had been completely unaware of her presence.

"I wanted to see Jessica."

"So you had me drugged and kidnapped?"

"I didn't think you would just say yes."

"You're right," he said. "I wouldn't have."

"Sit your ass down," I said.

"You her new pimp?" he asked me. He sat back down in the chair.

"I don't do the pimp thing," I answered.

"So what is this all about? Kill a cop; make a name for yourself?"

"It's like the lady said, she wants to see the baby."

"Well, she's too fucking late. The baby's not a baby anymore."

"Whatever she is," Bev said, "I want to see her."

"Why, so you can fuck up her life, too?"

"She's my *child.*"

"She *was* your child. She's *my* child now."

"Shut up, you two," I stuck in, "where's the girl now?"

"I ain't telling you shit."

"Suit yourself," I said, "but sooner or later, she's going to start wondering where her father is."

He thought about that for a moment. "What are you going to do?"

"To her? Nothing except reintroduce her to her mother."

"Are you going to let her see me like this?"

"No, not unless you want me to."

He thought about that for another moment. "Are you going to kill me?"

"Not unless I have to," I said. I knew I was lying.

That's when I decided to really fuck with his head. "I'm the one who raped her," I said. "That's my baby she's carrying."

He didn't believe me. "You're lying," he said.

"Okay, I'm lying."

Bev looked at me askance. "You are lying, aren't you?"

"Yeah," I said, "I'm lying."

Bev seemed to accept that. But Avel wasn't so sure. "Prove it," he said.

"You want me to tell you how it went down?"

"Yes," he said, "tell me how it went down."

"Okay," I said, "you asked for it, you got it."

I told him that I learned who he was after he killed the kid up on Lunt. I didn't want to tell him that I had learned about him from Bev in the tavern over on Broadway. In an odd way, it was like I was protecting her identity. I told him it was easy. Everybody in the neighborhood knew about it. Everybody knew his name. I used a library computer to do a search on his name, and learned his address. He lived west on 55th Street out by Midway Airport in a little red brick bungalow. The grass was immaculately manicured, and the hedges had been clipped into those disgusting little balls. The only thing that separated his house from all the other houses on the block were the pink plastic flamingos flanking the front steps.

I told him that I watched his house for about two months. I learned when he and Jessica left and returned. I learned when they ate. I learned when they went to bed. I followed her to school. I figured out that on days when she was late for school, she cut through an alley behind the 7-Eleven about a block away.

Then I began to modify the story. I didn't tell Avel this, but my plan was to take pictures of her. My plan was to take pictures of a bad cop's daughter, and plaster them around the neighborhood where Avel had killed that kid. The caption was to read, "A Life for a Life."

On the day I finally planned to pull it off, I parked my car in that alley. I got there early, and, knowing Avel was already gone, I called their house from a cell phone I had just bought using phoney information. I wanted Jessica to answer, and I wanted to keep her on the line long enough to make her late for school so she would cut through the alley where I would be waiting with my camera.

She answered the phone. "Is that you, Mike?" she asked.

"No," I answered, "my name is . . .," and I gave her some bullshit name, the same one I used to get the phone, "and you've just won an all-expenses-paid . . ."

"Who the fuck are you kidding," she cut me off.

"But, . . ." I protested.

"Listen here," she said, "I don't give a shit what I've won. Right now I need to buy some shit, and you are wasting my time." She slammed the phone down.

I tried calling back, but the line was busy. I waited a couple of minutes, and called back again. The line was still busy. Figuring she would be late for sure, I crawled onto the back seat, and waited.

Sure enough, fifteen minutes later she came half running down the alley in my direction. She was gangly like a giraffe. Her knees seemed to rub together as she moved. I raised my camera and took pictures of her through the windshield, about six of them. Then I ducked down so she wouldn't notice me as she loped by. I leaned down figuring she would pay no attention to me because of my tinted windows. I waited long enough to give her plenty of time to get all the way by. Then I raised up and peeked out. To my chagrin and surprise, she was standing right next to me. She was leaning on my car waiting for somebody. I had to be cool. I almost stopped breathing.

Just then, a skinny white kid with long stringy brown hair walked up looking around to make sure no one was following him. I got my camera up, and took a picture of him through the rear tinted window. I clung to the hope that she wouldn't hear the shutter. He paused for one second. He passed her something; she passed him something. I took the picture. Then he walked off in a hurry, eyes looking down. I took another picture. He turned the corner out of sight, but she lingered a moment inspecting the package he had slipped her.

I don't know what possessed me to do it. This was supposed to be as undercover as a spy operation. A completely secret capture of images to embarrass and scare a cop. But before I could stop myself, I pushed the button to lower the window.

"Your father is going to love these pictures," I said. I flashed her the camera. I felt like an idiot. I had completely blown my cover. And for what? Money? Ego? How about for nothing! But now I had to act as if I had her dead to rights. I faked a confident smile.

"Who *are* you?" she asked.

"I am your worst nightmare," I said. "Your father is going to kick your ass when he sees these."

She stood there a moment pondering her options. Then she grabbed the handle and opened the door. "Move over," she said.

I did. She slipped in and slammed the door. She sat pouting for another long moment. I wondered what she could possibly be thinking about, and even more about why I had even let her in the car. Then all at once, like a crazy woman, she reached down and pulled off her shoes. She hesitated, then lifted her butt off the seat and reached under her skirt and slipped off her panties. She wadded them into a little ball, and tucked them into her jacket pocket. She sat with her knees pinched together. She was so tense, the outline of her knee caps were white on her skin.

"What are you doing?" I asked.

"I need those pictures," she said.

"And you're prepared to . . .." I couldn't conceal the tone of disbelief in my voice.

"It doesn't matter," she said. "I'm already pregnant."

Now it was *my* turn to hesitate. "Was he the father?" I turned my head in the direction Mike had scurried away.

She nodded yes. "If *you* fuck me, I can say I was raped."

"Until the baby is born," I said. "After that, it'll be pretty obvious that it wasn't me."

"If I'm raped, he'll agree to let me get an abortion."

"You hope," I said.

"Yes," she nodded, "I hope."

It was at that point that reason finally decided to prevail. "Get out of the car," I said.

"What?" Now it was her turn to fail to hide the disbelief in her voice. She looked me square in the face and said it again. "What?"

"Get out of my car."

"But what about the pictures?" she asked.

I reached over and opened the door. Then I pushed her into the alley. "These pictures aren't your concern," I said. Then I crawled back into the driver's seat, and started the engine. As I pulled away, I could see her in the rearview mirror hopping on one foot to get her shoe back on.

That's what really happened. I told Avel the modified version, that I snatched her into the car and fucked her for an hour. I told him that I fucked her in the ass until she bled. Then I told him that I stuck my dick in her mouth with flecks of shit still hanging from the head. I told him that she gagged on my come, and that I made her swallow it. Then the *coup de grâce*. I flipped him the pictures I had taken of her in the alley, and I laughed. "I wasn't after her," I said, "I was after you. This moment today is the one I wanted to savor. I wanted you to feel the pain."

"But why? I never did anything to you." He was struggling to hold back the tears.

"You said it yourself," I answered. "You killed that kid in the alley with Macklin. You lynched Duc. You killed a dozen black boys on a whim. Now it's your turn."

Bev didn't even bother to try to hold back the tears. She cried openly. But as she began to understand the gravity of the situation she had helped put herself into, her breathing quickened. "And now you have to kill us both," she said.

"I'm afraid so," I answered.

"But why?" Avel asked again. "What is this *really* about?"

"It's about ice cream," I said.

"Ice cream?!" There was a note of wonderment in his voice. It was as if he could see that the magic solution to his predicament had just been delivered to him, and he was beginning to believe in miracles. He didn't– in fact, couldn't– understand the reference. And I could tell that he was feverishly turning over in his mind the best way to explain that ice cream had nothing to do with anything, and that I should, therefore, let him live.

"You were out of control," I said. "*America* is out of control. I'm simply taking control back."

"Killing me and Bev is taking control back?" He had given up on the ice cream argument.

"Cops in this country today are surly, arrogant, rude, armed, dangerous, and drunk with power. Killing you is simply blunting an instrument of the state. Killing Bev is collateral damage."

"But I helped you," Bev said. "I helped you get him here."

"And I want to thank you for that," I said. "And killing you was never a part of the original plan."

"I'm the one who led you to Macklin in the first place."

"I know, I know. Your help has been invaluable."

"And this is the way you repay me?"

"So why this scheme?" Avel asked. "You could have killed me a long time ago. Why all this talk, all these questions?"

"I needed to be sure," I answered.

"Sure of what?"

"That you deserved to die."

"Are you sure now?"

"Yeah," I said, "I'm sure." I squeezed the trigger. The Glock didn't even jump. For a fleeting moment, I felt sorry for Jessica. I remembered her sitting in the car, her panties in her hands, squeezing her bony little knees together. But then I thought about it. Her father was an idiot, and got what was coming to him. I was doing that child a favor. Now she'd be able to get that abortion.

Bev dropped to her knees, and clasped her hands together under her chin. "Please, don't kill me," she said. "I'll do anything. *Anything!*" She waddled towards me on her knees. "I'll give you money. I'll . . ."

"Stand up," I said.

She sank deeper into her prayer position, her head bowed low.

"I said, stand up."

I could smell her begin to sweat. She heaved herself onto one foot, then onto the other, then pushed herself upright. Not all the way upright, but mostly. Her head and shoulders were still bent low.

"Jessica needs someone to look after her," I said. I couldn't believe what I was saying. I was supposed to be shooting her, and I was letting her go. "She wants an abortion. I want you to help her get one."

"I will," she said. "I will, I will."

The rest was easy. I set fire to the garage to destroy any evidence that the cops might try to recover. I dropped Bev off at home, and I left.

It was on. The war was on. And I had just won the first battle.

XVI

They say a man becomes what he dreams. I recently dreamt I was very powerful. In the dream, it was night, and I used the cover of darkness to jump fantastic distances. I dreamt I could jump across the street. I could jump over garages. And I spent a large part of the dream trying to prove I wasn't dreaming. I thought the dream was real, and I wanted to prove that I really could jump like Superman. Maybe I ate too much for dinner.

When I woke up and discovered that my powers were gone, I was disappointed.

Then I wrote it all down, as much of it as I could remember, and tried to analyze it. Did I feel powerless in my life, and dream of power to compensate? More often than not, my dreams meant nothing. This dream, however, haunted me. I couldn't shake the feeling that it was some kind of omen. I had to almost resist the urge to go get fitted for a red, yellow or blue cape. Or maybe that was a part of the dream, too.

In the dream, I wanted to call myself Captain something. Probably because for me, names were a big thing. I'd used so many of them over the years that I hardly knew who I was anymore. At least, that's how it used to be. Deep down, however, you never forget. Or maybe it's the other way around. Maybe we always forget, and think that remembering a name is the same as remembering a man.

Anyway, one day I woke up, and realized that the man and the moniker were different. The man could change the moniker as often as he changed underwear, and he would still be the same. That's when I decided that all I really needed was a code name, a name that I could use to refer to the core of the man, the entity that rode around in the vehicle to which ordinary names referred.

In fact, that was the crux of the issue. We tend to think that the man *is* the machine. The moniker names the machine, and we think it names the man. The lesson I learned was that the man had no name. *I* had no name.

I decided to pick one. I turned it into a project. I wanted something that truly reflected who I was. But it dawned on me that the project was the machine's project, not the man's. The man didn't need a project. The man didn't need anything. And given that the machine had no way of directly knowing the essence of the man, there was no way for the machine to name what the man truly was. So I decided to let the machine name the mission that the man performed through the machine.

Then it became simple. The machine knew what it did at the man's behest. It killed people. The man would identify the person, and the machine would kill it. Some of the persons were big; some of them were small. Some of them required cunning, some merely brute force. *All* of them required secrecy, before and after each job.

The man was a messenger of God, known and yet unknown. The man was a sign, unlucky for all to whom he pointed. The man was Death. The machine did his bidding, and the machine named the man Ophiuchus, the thirteenth sign, the thirteenth day, the thirteenth apostle. I liked it.

One of the things about getting old was that you took the time to reflect. I reflected often on who and what I was as a young man, and the more I reflected, the more I liked. The young me had flaws, but he also had something else. Or maybe youth simply looks better through the lens of forty years. What I had back then was idealism, hope. I actually believed that what I did could make a difference. Today, it's not the same. I do now what I started back then, but now it's just another job. I picked guys, and I killed them. Ho-hum. I rarely saw any change in the world that resulted from the kill.

This job, though, the one that I was considering now, could be different. For this job, I would have to convert to Judaism. I would have to study the Torah, the Talmud and the Kabbalah. This hit would be more political than some of my other ones. Or not. These days, all my hits had a political angle. But this one could be especially satisfying. This one would be a Head of State. This one would be Nostradamus' third Antichrist. This one would save the world. This one would be the Prime Minister of Israel, and I would have to convert to Judaism in order to get close to him.

This is the hit I'd been preparing for all my life. I am the Buddha; the Prime Minister of Israel is the Antichrist, the ultimate Avel. He knows I'm here, and he knows what I must do. It's physics. Matter and antimatter. Only in this case, only he will cease to exist, and the world will be saved.

I learned who he was by accident. It had been several months now, but after the fire, after Jiqin disappeared, after shooting Avel, I wanted to see Ida. I wanted to tell her that it was okay what she did, what *we* did. Our actions, as do all actions, stand alone. Without preamble. Without apology. Without explanation. Any preamble, any apology, any explanation would be irrelevant. They would be attributes piled upon attributes. I wanted to tell her that she didn't have to be crazy. She didn't have to be sorry. She didn't have to explain.

I went out to Kankakee to see her. They told me she had been released years earlier. They had no address or phone number. I had no idea where to begin looking. I tried to remember our time together, but memories fade over time. Even bad ones. I could scarcely remember how she looked anymore. Memories morphed into impressions, and impressions shifted among themselves until I could no longer be sure what was a true memory, and what was something I wish had happened.

I tried to remember her voice. I tried to remember the patterns of her speech. They were gone. They were all gone.

Then one day, she was there. I was heading somewhere– to the store, to the cleaners, who knows?– and I was riding the elevator down to the lobby. I stepped off, and pushed the glass inner door open on my way out. And there she was. She was standing there studying the directory. She was older now, as was I. Her hair was white and cut close like a man's. It formed a half inch thick layer of fuzz all over her head. I could still see in her the young woman that had gotten her first natural and had joined the Black Legion years earlier. Her skin was weathered some, but the young woman was still there staring at me over a distance of what, four decades?

"I knew I would find you," she said.

"I didn't know you were looking," I said back.

"You look good," she said. I knew she was lying.

"You look the same," I said, and I wasn't lying.

"So, which of these bells is yours?"

"The one with Jay Sam Guy."

"I see," she said. "Al Pearsons is Jay Sam Guy."

"Al Pearsons is dead," I said. "How did you find me?"

"I followed you from the hospital."

I took her back upstairs to the apartment, and made some tea. I thought she had always liked sassafras, but she asked for peppermint.

I guess I was trying to make it like it used to be, but it wasn't the same. We weren't in love any more, and being there with her felt like being with a stranger, a stranger that I somehow recognized.

"So, how are you?" I asked. I didn't want to ask if she was still crazy.

"Still crazy," she said as if she had been reading my mind, "just better able to control it."

I pondered for a long moment the events of that evening so many years ago, events I hadn't pondered much since they happened. I remembered the feel of the gun in my hand and the recoil as I fired it, the smell of the gasoline as we threw the Molotov cocktails into the corners of the room, the red streaks of blood on the wall. I remembered the look on Ida's face as we raced away from the scene, and shortly before she began to vomit away our child in dry heaves that became vaginal bleeding that led to her miscarriage. "We did the right thing," I said.

"I've already forgiven myself," she announced.

"Have you forgiven me?" I asked.

She hesitated for a moment, then said, "I've been following your career."

"That's not possible," I said.

"Anything is possible."

I didn't want to let on that I had continued over the years killing people. At the same time, I wanted to know what she thought she knew. "I lived in the streets for years after that night," I said.

"Really?" she said. It was a question, but it was really a statement. Her tone told me that she knew that I was beating around the bush.

She took a small sip of her tea, and smelled the aroma coming from the cup. "Good tea," she said. She was making light of my trying to be coy.

"I had a house for a while," I said.

"I know." She sipped some more tea. "It's a shame about that fire."

This conversation wasn't going like I had thought it would. "How did you . . .?"

"I've been following your career," she said again. She paused. Had she always paused like that, deliberately adding tension to the moment? I couldn't remember. Finally, she asked, "What do you know about the Antichrist?"

"Nothing," I answered. "What should I know?"

"You should know that he lives."

She *was* still crazy. I began to feel a little nervous. I mean, what if she started doing something? I began looking around the kitchen for things I could use as weapons. I'd heard that crazy people can have incredible strength.

"You don't believe me, do you?" she asked.

"Why would you think that?" I didn't want to say anything that would provoke her.

"His name is Benjamin," she said. "Nathan Benjamin."

I knew this name. "Benjamin?!" I asked, "Nathan . . . Ha! Who? Nathan Benjamin? Woman, you *are* mad. Nathan Benjamin is the Prime Minister of Israel."

"Nathan Benjamin is the Antichrist." Her tone of voice carried a note of finality, as if to say that argument and discussion were futile. Facts were facts, and 'Nathan Benjamin is the Antichrist' was a fact.

I decided to try a different approach. "How did you come to recognize him?" I asked.

"I looked at where he is, the Middle East, and I looked at what he does. I looked at who he agitates to go to war with, Iraq, Iran, Syria. None of this is new! It has all been foretold." She seemed irritated with me for not myself seeing that which was so obvious to her. "Look," she said, "I researched Nostradamus and the Antichrist. The three relevant quatrains all pointed to Benjamin. I began to wonder why no one else could see that which was so obvious. Was I some kind of genius? Was I the only one who could see it? Benjamin was born under a water sign in the Middle East, and came to power the same year a comet was sighted. What could be more obvious?"

She reached into a straw shoulder bag she was carrying, and pulled out a laminated card with the three quatrains. She read the first one,

"Century 1, Quatrain 50

"From the three water signs will be born a man

"who will celebrate Thursday as his feast day.

"His renown, praise, rule and power will grow

"on land and sea, bringing trouble to the East."

She sat on the edge of her chair so that I could see the card as she read from it. "The three water signs are Cancer, Scorpio and Pisces. Benjamin was born on March 21 under the sign of Pisces.

"Century 2, Quatrain 30

"One who the infernal gods of Hannibal

"Will cause to be reborn, terror of all mankind

"Never more horror nor the newspapers tell of worse in the past,

"Than will come to the Romans through Babel.

"This one means the third Antichrist will be born on the continent where Hannibal was born, Africa. Benjamin was born in Israel, on the continent of Africa.

"Century 2, Quatrain 62

"Mabus then will soon die, there will come

"A horrible slaughter of people and animals:

"At once vengeance is revealed coming from a hundred hands,

"Thirst and hunger when the comet will run.

"This one is the one that points to him coming into power the same year a comet is sighted. As it happens, a new comet was discovered the same year Benjamin came to power. It's as plain as the nose on your face."

"Not all of us have had the opportunity to study what you have studied," I said.

Begrudgingly, she conceded me that one little point.

"Besides," I continued, "it doesn't make sense."

"Nothing does," she countered.

"Well," I disagreed, "some things *do* make sense."

"*Nothing* makes sense," she asserted again.

"Sure it does," I defended. "There is an order to life and existence."

She laughed so hard, she almost dropped her tea. After she regained control, she said, "You always were a fool until something brought you around. Last time, it took a raid on the Black Legion office and the death of our friends to bring you around. What will it take this time?"

I felt offended. Then I remembered that I was dealing with a crazy woman. "Okay," I said, "explain yourself."

"The world is hooked on logic," she began. "The problem is that logic doesn't accurately map the universe, nor anything in it. We expect that *modus pones* and *modus tollens* will explain dark matter, dark energy and the primordial soup, but nothing could be further from the truth."

"It doesn't explain everything," I interjected, "but it explains a lot."

"It explains nothing," she continued. There was a tone of contempt in her voice. "For example, we assume that if the universe is expanding, it must have begun from something that was previously contracted. However, the primordial soup– the stuff from which the expansion began– was everywhere when it started expanding. Naturally, the question arises: What space is the soup expanding into? If it began everywhere, there is nowhere for it to expand into.

"Being wed, as we are, to the seeming infallibility of logic, we begin wrestling with the conundrum of somewhere coming into existence from nowhere."

"But that's a genuine problem," I said.

"It gets worse," she said, pretending she hadn't even heard me.. "As we peer deeper into space, searching for light from the big bang, we never realize that for some observable universe, we *are* the first light for which *they* are searching.. First light is everywhere. In other words, we needn't look into space to see the beginning of time. We need merely to look here where we are. Our research instrument should be a microscope, not a telescope."

She paused to sip some tea. I began to wonder what they could possibly have been feeding her in that hospital.

"Consider this," she started up again. "Our observable universe forms a globe around us that is like a glass marble with the earth in the middle, and the surface of the marble is moving away from the center at an increasing rate. That's where the notion of Dark Energy comes from. We assume there is an energy causing this increased rate of expansion. Eventually, that rate of expansion will approach the speed of light. If we were to conduct an Einsteinian experiment, and imagine that we were transported instantly to the surface of our marble, we would be at the center of a new marble that now had the earth on its surface. The earth would now be moving away from our new center, and the far edge of the earth's marble– now invisible to us– would be moving away from us at twice the rate that the earth is moving away."

"I'm not sure I'm following you," I said.

"Now move to the far edge of the new marble," she said, again ignoring me completely, "and we'll be at the center of a third marble. If we continue this process of transporting to the far edge of a new marble, we will arrive at a marble, call it marble zeta, from which the earth is moving at or near the speed of light. Marble zeta is a given distance from earth. We'll call that distance zeta. Now if we strike radii from earth of length zeta in all directions, and put a marble at the end of each radius, we would form a crystal orb consisting of countless new marbles around the earth's marble. The single most unique feature about the crystal orb would be that every point on it would be moving away from the earth at or near the speed of light. Similarly, the earth's marble would be moving away from every point on the crystal orb at or near the speed of light."

"Marble schmarble," I said under my breath, knowing she would ignore me.

She did.

"So what does this all mean?" she asked. "It means that the crystal orb is moving in all directions at the speed of light. It also means that opposite sides of the crystal orb are moving away from each other at the speed of light. This is the point at which logic breaks down!" She began to become animated with her own story. "Logic would dictate that opposite sides of the crystal orb are moving away from each other at twice the speed of light. Since, however, the speed of light cannot be exceeded, we are stuck with the notion that the speed of light is equal to twice the speed of light."

Now, for the first time, I was beginning to see the problem.

"If the speed of light is equal to twice the speed of light," she continued, "the rules of logic are completely out the window, and anything else imaginable can follow. Space can simultaneously expand and contract, and is at once nowhere and everywhere. From this simple construct, up is down, down is up, and everything is everything." She drained her tea, set the cup down on the table, and sat back looking me straight in the eye, almost daring me to confront her.

I could sense that she knew her story sounded like a crock of shit, but she didn't care. She had obviously spent a lot of time thinking about it, but my only response was, "Interesting. Very interesting." I was not going to confront a crazy woman.

"So there you have it," she said. "It is the light barrier that provides Dark Energy. Since the speed of light is constant, two objects moving away from each other at what ought to be twice the speed of light cause the space between the objects to fold in on itself. Distance cannot increase, so space increases by folding. Dark Energy is light unable to go any faster, thus folding space."

"And everything is everything," I repeated.

"Well," she said, "that, too. But the real point is that nothing makes any sense."

"And from that, I should pop Benjamin?"

"Yes, because it makes no sense."

"That and he is the Antichrist," I said.

"Well, yeah, that, too," she said.

Clearly, Ida was deranged. I wanted her gone, but I couldn't think of a graceful way to arrange it. I had to chuckle at myself. I could get rid of people for other people, but not for myself.

"So, how did you become so interested in astronomy?" I asked after what seemed like an awkwardly long pause.

I had expected a straightforward answer. It was, after all, a straightforward question. Instead, she looked at me kind of sheepishly.

"I don't know if I should tell you that," she answered.

How could I have possibly struck a nerve? I thought it, but I didn't say it. Instead, I asked with as level a voice as I could muster, "Why not?"

She giggled. "You might think I'm crazy for real."

"I already do," I said, "so you've got nothing to lose."

She paused again, then said, "I've seen them."

"Them?" I asked.

"Yes," she answered.

"Them who?" I asked.

"You know," she said. "*Them.*"

I knew what she meant, but I didn't believe her. I *couldn't* believe her. After all, *they* were not real. Again, however, I didn't want to provoke a crazy woman. "When was this," I asked.

"A long time ago," she said, "when I was a shorty."

I gestured with my hand in little circles to urge her to continue.

"Okay, okay," she said, then paused. She took a deep breath to gather her nerve. "It was back in 1954, maybe '55. It was summer time. We were visiting some people over on 15th and Drake. I don't remember why. That part isn't important. I was outside playing hopscotch with some other kids. Apropos of nothing, I looked up into the western sky. It was a clear day, about five in the afternoon. The sun was already behind the church across the street, and I saw this thing up in the air."

"Thing?" I asked.

"I know, I know," she said. "I'm getting there." She took another deep breath. "It was about the size of a small car, a VW maybe, shaped like a vitamin pill or a football with the ends pushed round. I got the attention of one or two of the kids I was playing with to look at it, but they blew it off as just a blimp. But it wasn't just a blimp. It had smoke coming out the back. In fact, that's what tipped me off. The smoke looked like cigarette smoke or the smoke coming out of the tail of a Flash Gordon rocket ship."

"I remember that smoke," I said. "That was some phony looking shit."

"Exactly," she said. "So I stared at it trying to figure out if they thought they were fooling somebody. In retrospect, I figured that they were monitoring our communications, but didn't know what they were seeing. They saw a Flash Gordon film, and thought that we thought it was real. So they mimicked it thinking that we would be fooled."

"Did it have wheels?"

"No wheels."

"Did it have wings?"

"No wings."

"So how was it staying up?"

"I don't know," she answered, "but stay up it did, cruising directly over the street at the height of a tall tree at about five miles per hour. It was moving so slowly, that I would take my turn lagging and hopping, and check back on it every couple of minutes. So I did that a couple of times. I'd get to sky blue, and check the blue sky. Then I noticed that something was different. It had an open windshield, and the light inside was a pastel green. Now, I started staring at it again. Just then, a head pops up from behind the dashboard, then ducks down again as if he was fixing something, or something."

"A head?" I asked.

"I'm getting there," she said. She was getting annoyed at my interruptions. "So now my thing is, fuck the game. I've got to look at this thing. So I'm staring, and it's easing along at a snail's pace. After a bit, he raises up again, and he's looking out over the street below him with an expression of satisfaction on his face like a farmer looking out over a field of ripening corn. Curious as to what he could possibly be looking at, I look down the street in the same direction he's looking."

"And?" I asked.

"And nothing. All I'm seeing is a bunch of black kids running, jumping, riding bikes and hollering at the top of their lungs. You know, doing what we do."

"That's it?"

"That's it. So now I'm looking back up at ole dude, and he looks over at me, then looks away. Then the motherfucker does a double-take, and looks back at me again." She does a double-take to demonstrate how ole dude did it. She looked like one of the Marx brothers doing one of their routines. "I mean, he stared me straight in the eye so long, I had time to ponder the notion of whether or not to wave at him. I had the distinct feeling that he was a friend, but I have no idea why. And just as I was about to raise my arm to wave, he ducked back down behind the dashboard."

I wanted to ask what it looked like, but decided against it.

"I'll never forget those grasshopper eyes," she said. "A tiny nose and a slit for a mouth, but huge dark eyes that sort of slanted up at the outside corners." She shook her head. "That's how I got interested in astronomy. Over the years, I kept waiting for information to come out about who they were or where they were from or something. I expected to see something in the newspapers. Eventually, I decided that if I was going to know anything about these critters, I would have to find out for myself. So, here I am."

"So what happened next?" I asked.

"Nothing. That's all I saw."

"So did the thing sail off into the sunset."

"That's all I saw," she said again. "When ole dude didn't come back up, I started lagging and hopping again. And when I looked back, it was gone. Poof."

"Just like that?"

"Just like that. Well," she paused, "there was one more little tidbit. A young brother who saw me desperately searching the sky trying to figure out how something that was moving at five miles per hour could already be gone told me he saw it streak straight up at about 5000 miles per hour."

"He said that?"

"He said it was faster than anything on this planet could go." She sat back, and put the empty cup to her lips as if finishing the last few drops of her tea. She set the cup on the table and pushed it away.

"More?" I asked.

"No," she said, "I'm straight." She paused a moment, then continued, "There is no question as to whether or not they exist. They do. I have seen them with my own eyes. Not lights in the clouds or cigars rocking the plane or any of that bullshit. I wasn't hypnotized or Spock-pinched. I was far enough away from him that he couldn't use any kind of mind erasing techniques on me. I saw what I saw, and I *know* what I saw. For me, the only question is: Why don't *they* want us to know they exist? I think it's because we have some history with these creatures, whoever they are. They are clearly not afraid of us. Their technology is way too advanced for them to be afraid of anything we can do. No," she said, and nodded her head slowly, "they want us ignorant for a reason, and we need to know what that reason is."

"So do you think that governments around the world are covering it up?" I asked. I wasn't sure where I was going with that line of questioning.

"Fuck if I know," she said, "and fuck if I care. I *know* what the truth is. I don't need to have it validated by somebody's president, ours or anybody elses." All at once, she jerked up straight in her chair. "I almost forgot the real reason I came here," she said. She reached into her straw shoulder bag again, and pulled out a manilla envelop. She stood up and handed it to me. "Read this after I leave," she said.

"Why can't I read it now?"

"Because now you're seeing me to the door."

"You're leaving?" I asked.

"I'm already gone," she answered. She turned, and scurried to the door.

I had barely enough time to catch the door as it was closing behind her. I had wanted to say something about it being nice to see her again and hoping we could catch up or something like that. But by the time I managed to get the door open again while fumbling with the envelope she had just given me, she was already stepping onto the elevator that apparently was already there waiting for her.

I slowly closed the door, then examined the envelope. It had the name Al Pearsons scribbled on the front. I hadn't remembered that her handwriting was so illegible. I only knew what it said because I knew only what it could have said. It looked more like 'All Persons' than 'Al Pearsons' giving the impression that the contents were meant for everyone, not merely for me. I opened it, and pulled out the sheets. I read the document:

The Ruleless Manifesto

I am a (wo)man of the universe. I make my own rules. There are no other rules to which I am bound. As such, I owe allegiance only to myself and to humanity. I herewith disavow any and all pledges and debts of any and all kinds to any and all states, governments, religions, corporations, and groups whose sole purpose is to perpetuate their own existence, or to exploit mankind individually or collectively. Aside from my own rules, I answer only to the laws of God. My relationship with God is my concern alone. I will allow no man or woman to define my relationship with God. Only I will interpret God's commandments to me. Only I will be responsible for carrying out those commandments, and only I will be accountable if I should fail. To the extent that I answer to the laws of man, I do so only as an expedient. I will never allow the laws of man to encroach in any meaningful way on my beliefs or goals. I will travel when and where I see fit, and learn what I choose to learn when I choose to learn it. I understand that, despite lofty pronouncements to the contrary, the laws of man were designed to control and stifle me rather than free and enrich me, and that if I am to get justice, I will have to resort to measures outside the domain of the laws of man to get it. I am fully prepared to do exactly that. I recognize individuals and associations as I see fit. I will associate with whomever I choose at whatever time or place is mutually agreeable to us so long as I and that other person are not taking undue advantage of the other owing to inexperience, youth, or poverty, and I vow to resist– directly or indirectly– the enslavement– physical, financial, psychological, emotional, or otherwise– of myself or others as an *a priori* obligation of my universality. Of necessity, my adherence to the Ruleless Manifesto will be kept secret. I will use the same Rules of Engagement when dealing with states, governments, religions and corporations as they use in dealing with me. In other words, I will always keep my own self interest and the interest of humanity paramount. If need be, and to the extent that I can get away with it, I will lie in order to get the state, government, religion or corporation to act more in my interest or in the interest of humanity. Together, states, governments, religions, and corporations strive to form a new world order where people are cattle to be consumed as food. States, governments, religions, and corporations are the enemy of the people, and I will always, always, always fight them tooth and nail. I understand that the best way to fight them is to target their leaders and sometimes their employees. I will teach my children to understand the principles of the Ruleless Manifesto. I will teach them *how* to think rather than *what* to think. I will help them to understand why to never trust states, governments, religions or corporations of any kind, nor any of their minions. I will teach them the skills to survive by any means necessary. I will never subjugate my will to the will of any state, government, religion, or corporation. My only duty will always be to God, humanity, and myself. I am– and always will be– my own (wo)man and only authority.

She had spent a lot of time working on this. It was as carefully drafted as my 'MY LIFE' document. Ironically, it looked as if she had used the same kind of paper I had used. She used sheets of clean, white, acid-free, 25% cotton fibre, 24 pound bond that had the manufacturer's watermark emblazoned in the middle, a round circle with a winged dragon clutching a ribbon banner with the manufacturer's name in calligraphic script. She had even used the same color ink. I tried to resist my natural inclination towards paranoia, but I couldn't. She said she had been following my career, but this was so me, it looked like she had been following me for years. She knew what was in my head. She was good. She was too good.

I slipped over to the front windows, pulled back the drapes, and peeked out, hoping to see I wasn't sure what. I saw an old man across the street jogging north. He looked as if every step was a chore that maybe he wasn't sure he was up to. I saw a bat darting to and fro between the buildings just beyond the old man jogging. It struck me that I had never seen a bat in this neighborhood before, and I wondered what it was doing out in broad daylight. I saw a bus cruise south in front of my apartment building. I knew that Ida was on it, but knowing she was gone didn't make me feel any less ill at ease. I couldn't shake the feeling that she simply knew too much about me.

XVII

I didn't see Miss Abbey again until Cop Buck's funeral. Apparently, someone beat him to the gun he had placed on the table, and shot him in the face.

Grandma Daughter's take on it was that only a fool would play such a dangerous game anyway, and that he got his due. Mama simply felt sorry for Miss Blue.

It was Mama who first put the notion in my head.

"I didn't know her last name was Beaman," she said, listening to the eulogy.

I, however, *did* know her name was Beaman. And I knew her maiden name was Carpenter.

"So why did people call her Miss Blue?" Mama asked.

Why indeed?

Later, at the cemetery, I looked over at Miss Blue and Miss Abbey standing near a gaping hole in the ground where the "big and gorgeous and sweet" Sydney was about to be deposited. Miss Blue wore an ankle-length black dress that looked like it was covered with ruffles. It looked like it could be a party dress except this wasn't a party. She also wore a wide brim black hat with a black veil that looked like a mosquito net.

Miss Abbey stood right next to her with her arm around Miss Blue's shoulders, their bodies pressed against each other.

There were only a few people milling around in the grass that surrounded the hole. Half of them were police officers with whom Sydney had worked. As they began to drift away from the grave site, I pulled away from Mama long enough to get closer to Miss Blue, but especially to Miss Abbey.

"I'm sorry, Miss Blue," I said.

She eased away from Miss Abbey, and pulled me close to her. "Thank you, honey," she said. "You're so sweet."

Then, almost as if I were on automatic pilot, I went over and hugged Miss Abbey. I literally grabbed her around the waist and buried my face in her abdomen.

"Oh-h-h," she said, "I missed you, too." She placed her hand on my head.

I knew somehow that this was going to be the last time I saw her. So I took one long deep breath hoping against hope to gather that wonderful smell. It wasn't there. The air was thick with the smell of freshly dug soil, and the only images I could conger were those of earthworms.

When I released my embrace, I stepped back over to Miss Blue. "Why do they call you Miss Blue?" I asked.

The abruptness of the question took her aback. She laughed, and pulled the veil from in front of her face. She pulled it back over the top of her hat. There was a rosiness in her cheeks that I had never seen before.

"Sydney's the one who started that," she said. "Or maybe it was one of his friends. To them, I was too pale, too . . . blue."

"You don't look blue to me," I said.

Miss Abbey chortled, "She's not any more." She put her arm around Miss Blue's shoulders again, and Miss Blue put her arm around Miss Abbey's waist. They pulled each other close.

As they turned to leave, I felt Mama take my hand into her own. We walked in the opposite direction, but, looking back over my shoulder,

I watched Miss Blue and Miss Abbey walking away for as long as I could. And even at that expanding distance, I found myself breathing in just a little bit deeper, just a little bit longer.

My hunch was right. I never saw either of them again. Some time after the funeral, I overheard Grandma Daughter telling Mama that Sydney wasn't killed in a bar fight after all. She found out that he shot himself in the face while cleaning his service revolver at home. It was her opinion that Miss Blue shot him, and that all the stories that circulated about what happened were simply gossip started by it-was-anybody's-guess.

Mama disagreed. She thought that if either of them shot him, it was Miss Abbey. I was surprised to hear that Mama never liked the look of Miss Abbey, anyway. To Mama, Miss Abbey looked like a sneak, someone who couldn't be trusted. Since I had crossed my heart and hoped to die, I couldn't correct Mama. I couldn't tell her that Miss Abbey was a wonderful person with a wonderful smell. And back then, I couldn't know it, but it was Miss Abbey's fault. It was her fault that it would be years before I could look at a white woman even in a magazine and not wonder what it would be like between her legs.

XIII

After Ida left, I went through the whole house looking for surveillance plants. I had equipment that would detect bugs of various kinds, and I scanned every nook and cranny of the apartment. I found nothing. I checked the proximity of neighboring structures to make sure that I wasn't being reconnoitered from a distance. I recalculated satellite movements to make sure they couldn't be used to spy on my abode. Again, I found nothing.

After that, I must have read the Manifesto a dozen times, line by line. Then I began to wonder whether or not she could have guessed a lot of what she had there about me. We did, after all, live together once. Maybe she was able to extrapolate from what I had been to what I had become. It seemed unlikely, but how else could she have come up with such a condensed– no, distilled– account of the essence of my being. Are we really like acorns that contain the essence of the tree? I never thought so before, but now I wasn't sure.

I read the first few lines again, this time aloud,

"I am a man of the universe. I make my own rules.
There are no other rules to which I am bound. As such,
I owe allegiance only to myself and to humanity."

What does that even mean? I knew, and yet, I didn't know. People on earth are born into societal structures determined by country, race, gender, economic status, who knows what all? But to become a universal person meant to transcend all that. It meant to be more than all that. I tried to remember what in my childhood could have led me to become who I was. It struck me almost instantly.

I was a freshman at Hyde Park High School. It was near the end of my freshman year, so it was in the late spring. My friends and I would eat lunch every day in the park across Stony Island Avenue. We were young, so we ate, told jokes, postured for the girls, tried to act cool. It's what we did, and I did what was expected of me.

But there was one student there who did not do what was expected. I didn't know how old he was, but I suspected he was at least old enough to be a senior. He came to school every day dressed in a business suit, white shirt, tie and black lace-up leather shoes. That in itself was odd for a black boy in that day and time. The rest of us were trying to be Ivy League cool wearing khaki pants with buckles in the back or gangster tough with high-crown hats and long collar shirts. He fit into none of the cliques of the day.

His lunch period was the same as mine, so I saw him every day. But he never crossed over into the park with the rest of the students. He always stayed near the building, and he was always accompanied by the same two white girls. They were one blonde and one brunette, and they were also always dressed to the nines. They wore lacy, pastel blouses, short, tight skirts that accented the curve of their butts, stockings and leather pumps, sometimes black, sometimes blue, sometimes red.

I never once saw any one of the three of them talking to another student. They always kept to themselves.

Naturally, I wanted to know who they were. In truth, I was envious. I secretly wished that my parents had the kind of money their parents had. The three of them looked too old to be students, yet too young to be teachers, and I always wanted to know what their relationship to one another was. They didn't follow the rules. They weren't like us. It was 1956, and blacks and whites didn't hang together like that then, not there, not at Hyde Park High. Not that *I* knew about. It wasn't done. Yet, there they were.

One young sister in our crowd openly scoffed, "Look at him with *two* of 'em. You *know* what they doing."

I *didn't* know what they were doing, but I didn't want to look like a square, so I nodded and said, "Um-hum."

Before the semester was over, they stopped showing up around school. After about a week, the same sister said, "See, I *told* you."

I nodded and said, "Um-hum," again.

In truth, I had no clue. But it intrigued me that he could do what he did, namely, whatever he wanted. At least, that's how it appeared. Secretly, I vowed to be like him. I vowed to be my own kind of man, answerable to no one.

In my mind, this boy had achieved the unachievable. At his age, people were telling stories about him. He was already a legend. I imagined that his name was Shane or Hammer or Gunn, something that a legend would be called, something that would strike fear in mens hearts at its very mention. Maybe this was the Genesis of my placing so much importance on names.

I imagined a gypsy woman telling the story of a young boy befriending a snake. The boy woke up one morning with the snake coiled up and resting on his chest. Over time, the boy learned how to call the snake with a special whistle. The snake would come, and the boy would feed it cornbread. One day, the snake attacked the boy's mother, and the mother threatened to kill the snake. But the gypsy woman warned that if the mother killed the snake, she would also kill the boy. Like the boy at Hyde Park High– I think I settled on calling him Puck after some character in a Shakespearean play I was forced to read– the boy in my imagination had achieved a power over adults, a power over authority. *That* is what I wanted. *That* is what I was determined to have.

I read aloud the next couple of lines from the Manifesto.

> "I herewith disavow any and all pledges and debts of any and all kinds to any and all states, governments, religions, corporations, and groups whose sole purpose is to perpetuate their own existence, or to exploit mankind individually or collectively."

For me, this one was easy. Since I had lived on the streets of Chicago for so long, there was no record of me anywhere under my birth name. Maybe a birth certificate, but that would be it. I was like an alien in my own country of birth. But even now, now that I had an identity, now that I had a name, I still formed no official allegiances. I didn't make deals with entities whose eyes I could not look into.

These lines reminded me of my time in the U.S. military. I signed a contract to submit my will to the will of the government for a period of 4 years. And look how that turned out! I was wanted for a murder I hadn't even committed. Well, not me exactly. More like the entity that used to bear my birth name. But that was a long time ago. And as far as the U.S. government knew and would ever know, that entity was dead.

But the question remained, how did Ida know that about me? I looked back in my past for clues as to how I even became that way. It didn't take long before I remembered. It was in my sophomore year. I was sitting in front of the school. It was late in the afternoon. All the kids had already gone home. I didn't even remember why I was there that late. I do remember that the building was deserted. Maybe it was a Saturday or Sunday. Anyway, I was sitting by the front door, and a cop car rolls up in front of the school. The guy riding shotgun saw me, and gestured for the driver to pull onto the sidewalk and onto the verge of the building that led up to where I was sitting.

"What are you doing here, boy?" the guy riding shotgun asked.

"I go to school here," I answered.

"The school is closed."

Just then, the driver, apparently thinking my answer was insolent, got out of the squadral, came around and grabbed me up by my collar from where I was sitting on the steps, and smacked me in the face. He threw me against the hood of the car, then twisted my arm behind my back so hard, I thought he was trying to break it.

"What did I do?" I protested.

"Shut the fuck up!"

"But I didn't do nothing."

"I said, shut the fuck up!"

So, I shut the fuck up. He fumbled through my pockets pulling out all my little belongings, my coin purse, my wallet, my handkerchief, my keys. He threw everything except my wallet on the ground. He fished through that until he found the two dollar bill I had stashed in one of the secret pockets. He stuffed that into his own pocket. Then he read aloud my address from one of the cards I had in one of the cellophane windows.

"Is that your address?" he asked.

"Yes," I answered.

He pushed me away from him.

"Take your little, skinny ass home, before I have to kick it for real," he said.

"Can I get my keys," I asked.

He kicked the keys in my direction, then turned and signaled his partner that he was ready to leave. I scrambled to the ground, and I collected my things.

That was one of the first steps that I was forced to take along the road that led to manhood. I cried as I walked home feeling powerless, embarrassed, humiliated. I wanted to get even, but I had no clue how to go about it. I wondered what Puck would do. I bet he wouldn't be slinking home crying, mopping his nose on his sleeve. Puck would get even for real. Puck wouldn't give a fuck. Eventually, I pushed the incident from my mind. I pushed it aside, but I never forgot.

I read the next few lines aloud.

> "Aside from my own rules, I answer only to the laws of
> God. My relationship with God is my concern alone.
> I will allow no man or woman to define my relationship
> with God. Only I will interpret God's commandments
> to me. Only I will be responsible for carrying out those
> commandments, and only I will be accountable if I
> should fail."

It was Grandma Daughter that influenced me here. She was the one who introduced me to that book with the sphinx in it. I still remembered the portion of the caption that read: Hence the quaternary of the magi: KNOW, DARE, WILL, KEEP SILENT. I knew all too well that it meant that any man could be or have anything in the universe by simply knowing what he wanted, daring to have it, working towards it, and keeping quiet about it so no one would work against it. Moreover, one could want it all, be it all, be God. One could be absolutely and infinitely free, transcend the laws of man as well as those of nature. This part was a no-brainer. But the question remained, how did Ida know. I tried to remember having told her-- or anyone else for that matter– about the quaternary. I couldn't remember.

I read on.

"To the extent that I answer to the laws of man, I do so only as an expedient. I will never allow the laws of man to encroach in any meaningful way on my beliefs or goals. I will travel when and where I see fit, and learn what I choose to learn when I choose to learn it."

This one took some reflection. It had never come up as an issue that I had to concern myself with having been denied access to any meaningful knowledge. That's when I remembered Miss Beulah and Peter. They were husband and wife, and they lived not far from us when we lived over on the fifty-five hundred block of LaSalle. And as Miss Beulah constantly reminded Peter, the house they lived in belonged to her.

No two people on earth could have been more different. Miss Beulah was a high-yellow woman who was slow of mind, lazy of body, and fearful of spirit. She was short, just over five feet. She was fat. She weighed around two hundred and fifty pounds. And she rarely– if ever– got outside of her comfort zone.

One of the rare instances when she did was when she learned how to drive at the age of fifty. Peter taught her in a big, black, 1953 Buick Roadmaster sedan they owned. She was Grandma Daughter's friend, and she would, from time to time, offer to take us for a ride. We would all pile in, the two women in front and me in back, and Miss Beulah would drive four blocks in one direction along Garfield Boulevard, then turn around and drive four blocks back. She would carefully re-park the Buick, and get out.

"Whew," she would exclaim, "driving is hard work."

"But you did real good," Grandma Daughter would tell her.

Miss Beulah would beam, but I remembered wondering why we even bothered to get into the car at all given that we only drove about a mile. I was just getting comfortable about the time the ride was over. It always struck me as a waste of time.

Peter, on the other hand, was *my* friend. Well, he was friend*ly*. Maybe he saw himself in me, because I reckoned he thought Grandma Daughter ran me the way Miss Beulah ran him.

Miss Beulah kept Peter on a tight leash. Peter was tall, lean and black. He was smart, and he liked doing things, new things.

Miss Beulah and Peter argued in front of Grandma Daughter and me once.

"Your ass ain't gon' be riding no damn motorcycle."

"But, honey, . . ."

"But, honey, my ass. I said no, and I meant no."

It wasn't until Miss Beulah died that we learned the truth about Peter. Not only had he already learned how to ride a motorcycle, he also already *owned* one. He sold the Buick, dyed his hair black– it had turned almost all grey– and moved the woman he had been seeing for years before Miss Beulah died into Miss Beulah's house.

I ran into him about six months after Miss Beulah's death, and he must have seen in my eyes that I wanted to ask him how he did it. Without me saying a word, he smiled at me and said, "I do what I want to do, no matter what."

That was all he said, because that was all he needed to say. He knew that I understood him perfectly.

The next couple of lines were crystal clear.

> "I understand that, despite lofty pronouncements to the
> contrary, the laws of man were designed to control and

stifle me rather than free and enrich me, and that if I am to get justice, I will have to resort to measures outside the domain of the laws of man to get it. I am fully prepared to do exactly that."

I knew immediately how Ida knew about this part of my life. This part of my life was part of her life as well. It was this episode that drove her crazy. I wondered how she stayed sane enough to write about it here.

I read on.

"I recognize individuals and associations as I see fit. I will associate with whomever I choose at whatever time or place is mutually agreeable to us so long as I and that other person are not taking undue advantage of the other owing to inexperience, youth, or poverty, and I vow to resist– directly or indirectly– the enslavement– physical, financial, psychological, emotional, or otherwise– of myself or others as an *a priori* obligation of my universality."

I remembered Beck. At least, that's what he said people called him. I couldn't pronounce his real name, because it consisted of sounds and clicks that we don't have in English. He was a refugee from somewhere in Africa. I want to say Sudan, but it could have been anywhere. He may even have been a refugee in the last African country he was in.

I met him at a rally. Oddly enough, neither of us was participating in the rally. Odder still, the rally was in protest of the Israeli treatment of Palestinians in Gaza. People were walking in front of the Israeli consulate over on Wacker Drive at Michigan Avenue. There were only about a dozen protesters. One of them carried a blue and white placard that replicated the Israeli flag where the Star of David had been replaced by a pale blue swastika. They chanted 'End the Genocide' and 'Break the Blockade' almost nonstop.

I couldn't remember why I was in that area, but the commotion piqued my interest. I walked over, and as I passed the entrance to the garage, I saw Beck from the corner of my eye huddled next to the garage door. He was taller than me, maybe 6'3". And he was skinny like a waif from a war zone. He wasn't malnourished, he was just real skinny. And he was so black that his skin had a tinge of blue to it. He wore jeans and a peacoat, and he walked like a scarecrow as he approached me.

"Excuse me," he said. "Are you a part of the demonstration?"

He had a thick accent that I didn't recognize.

"No," I answered, "I thought *you* might be."

He chortled, "Not a chance. The Palestinians deserve anything the Israelis do to them."

"Then why are you here?" I asked.

"I'm just looking," he answered. "Maybe I thought I might change somebody's mind."

"About what?"

"About Israel."

"What about Israel?"

"The real question is, what about the Palestinians?" he said.

"Okay," I answered back, "what about the Palestinians?"

"I hope they all eat shit and die," he said.

"I got that part. The question is, why?"

"They don't belong there."

"They don't belong *where*?"

"In Africa!"

I was a little taken aback. "Okay," I said, "where should they be?"

"I don't know where they should be. I just know they took the land in North Africa by force centuries ago, and it is long past time for them to be gone."

"Aren't there laws that govern this kind of thing?" I asked.

"Look, . . . What's your name?"

"Jay," I answered.

"My name is . . .," then he made this sound with his mouth that resembled a click followed by a syllable that I didn't recognize. Then he said, "Folks here call me Beck."

"Hi, Beck."

"Look, Jay, . . ."

Just then, the cop who had been standing to one side monitoring the demonstration motioned us to move along. I guess he could tell that we weren't part of the protest.

"Why?" Beck asked. The passion of our conversation got transfered into his question to the cop.

I wanted him to be quiet, because I didn't want to draw attention in our direction.

"Because I said so," the officer answered. He was a young brother who wore dread locks under his service cap. He probably harbored the hope of doing undercover work one day infiltrating groups of artists or actors or musicians who created works that cried out for justice.

"But we're not doing anything," Beck protested. "We have rights."

"Your rights out here are what I say they are. And I just ordered you to move along. Now say something else so I can teach you not to fuck with a cop." He rested his hand on his nightstick, and flexed his fingers.

"Let's go, babe," I said to him. "This is a battle that is not worth fighting this time."

That's when the officer directed his attention to me.

"You need to be careful who you hang out with," he said. "I know this kind of person, and he is nothing but trouble."

"You don't know me!" Beck said.

"No, but I know your kind. I should call the immigration service on your ass. Where you from anyway?"

"Let's go," I said to him again.

"I am not leaving this place," he said. "I have a valid green card, and I have rights in this country."

All of this happened around the time Jiqin and her uncle were living with me in the three story apartment building I squatted in on Seventy-seventh and Lake Shore Drive. They stayed with me because they were illegal immigrants with fake green cards. I could not help but be reminded of Jiqin and her connections for getting fake identification cards.

I touched Beck on the arm in order to get his attention, but he yanked away from me.

"I warned you," the cop said to him. "You're under arrest."

"For what?" I asked.

"Don't do it, Jay," Beck said.

"You better listen to him," the cop said.

I thought about it. The last thing I needed was to get arrested. That possibility was already too close for comfort. So I did nothing. The cop escorted Beck to his squad car, and put him into the back seat. I hadn't known the man fifteen minutes, but he was already truly my friend.

I read some more.

> "Of necessity, my adherence to the Ruleless Manifesto
> will be kept secret. I will use the same Rules of

Engagement when dealing with states, governments, religions, and corporations as they use in dealing with me. In other words, I will always keep my own self interest and the interest of humanity paramount. If need be, and to the extent that I can get away with it, I will lie in order to get the state, government, religion, or corporation to act more in my interest or in the interest of humanity. Together, states, governments, religions, and corporations strive to form a new world order where people are cattle to be consumed as food. States, governments, religions, and corporations are the enemy of the people, and I will always, always, always fight them tooth and nail. I understand that the best way to fight them is to target their leaders and sometimes their employees."

At first blush, this one seemed obvious. But as I reflected on my past, I couldn't focus on any incident that embodied this principle, let alone an incident that Ida would know about. Then, I reflected on Inez Cooper, a woman I met on the bus from Atlanta, Georgia, to Chicago. I had just finished a job in Valdosta, and was on my way home.

"I definitely believe in miracles," she said. She was a southern woman, dark skin, straightened black hair. "I have seen them first-hand."

Her voice, as she talked, was like music. She modulated her tone higher at times, then lower, as if she were singing. I was nearly mesmerized just listening to her. She went on to explain that she and her sister, Mary, had years ago visited a holy shrine in the Middle East. While there, they witnessed a young boy about age seven crying as he watched an old woman weaving a basket. The woman told the boy that she would give him the basket if he returned to that same place again the next day.

Ten or twelve years later, Inez and Mary were driving along a street in Nashville, Tennessee, where numerous yard sales were taking place.

"Stop!" Mary shouted as they passed one paticular yard sale. "I think I see a basket."

"How can you see a basket when I'm driving at fifty miles an hour?" Inez asked her.

"Just turn around and go back," Mary said.

So she did.

As they approached the yard sale with the basket, they noticed a young man with dark, curly hair standing near it.

"How much for this basket?" Mary asked him.

"Five dollars," he replied. "But before I can sell it to you, I must get your name and address in case I want it back."

Mary gave him the information he wanted, and paid for the basket.

A month later, Mary's husband, Edward, was driving along some street in Nashville during a heavy rain storm. The street was littered with trash cans that had been blown over by the wind.

Edward stopped the car to remove one such can that was blocking his way. Under the can, he saw a painting of a vase with flowers. He thought Mary might like the painting, so he rescued it, and took it home. Mary cleaned the painting up, and displayed it in the hallway of her home.

Inez saw the painting with its yellows, whites, greens and browns, and was reminded of works by Renoir. She suggested that Mary have the piece examined by instructors at the Art Institute of Tennessee. Mary did, and they refered her to Sotheby's in New York. People from Sotheby's came to Nashville, and ultimately offered Mary and Edward over one million dollars for the painting. It was in fact a genuine Renoir.

Several months later, the boy from the yard sale showed up at Mary's door with five dollars to buy the basket back.

"Did it bring you luck?" he asked.

"You're the boy from the shrine," she said.

"The basket brings luck to anyone who owns it."

Inez ended her story there.

"That's a lot of money," I said. "The taxes on it must have been steep."

"Not if you cash it in Switzerland," she said. Her mouth turned up a Mona Lisa-like smile, more mysterious even than her voice, and equally mesmerizing.

I returned to the Manifesto.

> "I will teach my children to understand the principles of the Ruleless Manifesto. I will teach them *how* to think rather than *what* to think. I will help them to understand why to never trust states, governments, religions or corporations of any kind, nor any of their minions. I will teach them the skills to survive by any means necessary."

It was Grandma Daughter who came to mind again with this one. Not so much for something she said or did, but rather for something she would have said or done had the situation to do so arisen. She was her own woman, and had I asked her, she would have told me to be my own man. She would have told me to go where I wanted when I wanted for the reason I wanted, and not to allow anyone to stand in my way. She would have told me that because that was what *she* was. She didn't care what people thought about what she did. She did what she did because she wanted to do it. The candles, the books, the magic. All of it was stuff that ordinary people would avoid. Ordinary people would shy away from them because of the unsavory connotations associated with them. Not Grandma Daughter. The reasons other people would avoid them would be the very reasons Grandma Daughter would be drawn to them. She would want to know what it was about them that turned other people off. That was the way she was. That was the way *I* was.

I read the final passage.

> "I will never subjugate my will to the will of any state,
> government, religion or corporation. My only duty will
> always be to God, humanity and myself. I am– and
> always will be– my own (wo)man and only authority."

This one was a slam dunk. I could feel my pulse quicken as I read this piece, and that was enough to tell me that it resonated with me on a level beyond the intellectual. This passage caused a reaction down in the very core of my being. I had no option but to be it, my own man and only authority.

States, governments, religions and corporations don't like it, but their not liking it doesn't change the fact that there are some men to whom the laws of man do not apply. And depending upon the entity, they have various ways of dealing with such people. States and governments use prisons. Religions use the promise of an eternity in hell. Corporations rely on the laws they get passed in order to use states and governments to punish those who violate their rules. But the intent is always the same. Stifle those who don't do what they're told.

Maybe Ida was right after all. Maybe the world *is* hooked on logic, and rules are societies' way of making order out of chaos. The problem as they see it is that men need to be governed. And men who won't be governed-- men like me-- will be controlled, imprisoned or killed.

What they never take into account is that people like me might strike back. That's where we have the advantage. We can hide among the rules, and strike with impunity. Just then, the quaternary of the magi flashed into my mind: KNOW, DARE, WILL, KEEP SILENT.

XIX

It was weeks before I saw Ida again. Not that I was looking for her, but in fact I guess I was doing exactly that. I was paranoid again like I had been all those years that I spent living in the streets. And when she finally showed up, I was pissed off. She simply showed up one day in the lobby of my building like nothing was wrong and like it was cool for her to be there. The truth is, it *was* cool for her to be there. I just couldn't come to grips with the fact that she was able to drift in and out of my life these days completely undetected. *I* was supposed to be the one who was the professional here. Stealth was *my* business. Yet I never knew when and how Ida came and went.

"I'd like a cup of tea," she announced in a tone that made me feel like she considered me to be her man-servant or something. At the same time, I felt powerless to say no. I wanted to talk to her. I *needed* to talk to her. I needed to figure out how she knew about me what she knew.

"Sure," I said. I tried to sound strong, but I felt like a lap-dog. I was so completely discombobulated at seeing her standing in the lobby that I completely forgot the reason I was in the lobby in the first place. "Come on up. I'll fix some."

"You wouldn't have any green tea, would you?" she asked as we stepped onto the elevator.

"I don't drink green tea," I answered.

"Pick some up the next time you're at the store," she said. "My stomach's been bothering me lately, and I've heard green tea can help."

'Bitch' flashed through my mind, but I stifled it before it got to my lips. Foul language was no way to get from her information on how she knew what she knew.

Once upstairs, she excused herself and went to the bathroom. I could hear her in there taking a leak and washing her hands. I steeled myself to blurt out the question, but she cut me off as soon as she opened the bathroom door.

"I've already answered your question," she said. "You simply don't believe what I told you."

"Tell me again," I insisted.

"Saying it again won't change anything," she countered. "You still won't believe me."

"Try me."

"What do you know about epistemology?" she asked.

"episte-what?"

"I'll take that to mean not much."

"What *is* that?"

"Epistemology is the theory of knowledge. It seeks to answer the question of how we know what we know."

"And?" I asked.

"It's all bullshit," she answered.

I remembered the last conversation we had, and I wasn't going to fall for that same old ploy. I nodded my head in the affirmative.

"It's all bullshit," she said again.

I kept nodding.

She leaned over and shouted in my face, "Everything we know is bullshit!"

"Okay, okay, okay," I said. "We know nothing, nothing, nothing."

"That's a good start," she said. "But do you know *why* we know nothing, nothing, nothing?"

"Because we're stupid," I answered. My cause was completely lost, and I knew it.

"No," she said. "It's because it's impossible to know everything."

I didn't want to answer, but the words escaped anyway, "What is that supposed to mean?"

"There is stuff in the universe that is knowable, right?"

"Right."

"And we know some of it, right?"

"Right."

"For example, we know about the light spectrum, right?"

"Well, yeah, right." I was trying to anticipate where she was going with all of this.

"So, now the question," she said. "Was the light spectrum knowable before we knew about it?"

I had to think about that one. After reasoning that the laws of the universe are discovered, not created, I reasoned that the laws were there all along merely waiting. I answered, "Yes."

"In other words," she continued, "ancient man could have known about the light spectrum."

She said it like a statement, but it was really a question.

"Well, no," I said, "because he might not have had the intellect to understand it."

"What if you networked ancient men's minds?"

"It wouldn't matter," I answered. "The light spectrum was beyond them."

"Yes," she said. She sounded like a teacher emphasizing a point for a slow learner. She relaxed and sat back in her chair. "Yes," she said again.

I had expected her to say more, but she didn't. I waited a few more seconds, then said, "But now we do know."

"You're missing the next step," she said.

"What next step? We know what they didn't know."

She made that sucking click with her tongue that smart people make in the presence of slow people.

"Could ancient man have even *imagined* the light spectrum?"

"No," I answered.

She paused a long moment waiting for me to connect dots that clearly were not there.

Then she said, "The light spectrum was knowable, but they couldn't know it. Therefore, there is stuff out there that is knowable that *we* cannot know."

"Like what?" I asked.

"I don't know," she said. "Not only that, but I *can't* know. None of us can know. Moreover, we cannot even imagine that which we don't know. We can imagine only that which we can know. If we can't know it, we can't imagine it."

Now I understood her point.

"As we evolve," I said, "we'll know more until we know everything."

"No!" she said. "And that's the point I'm making. No matter how big the brain gets, there will be something out there beyond it's reach."

"Even if you network them," I said. I could hear the tone of resignation in my own voice.

"Now you see what I see," she said. "There is stuff out there that even ole dude in the Flash Gordon rocket ship cannot know. That is the nature of the universe." She paused for a long moment, then said, "You know that you're the new John Brown, don't you?" I thought this might be her round-about way of answering my original question of how she knew about me what she knew.

"What?" I said. I feigned having trouble coping with this sudden change in topic. "Don't call me John Brown. *I* am Jay Sam Guy."

"John Brown murdered for the cause of freedom."

"What's that got to do with me?"

She looked at me, and made that sucking click with her tongue again. She looked away. "Did you read . . .?"

"Yeah, I read it. So what?"

"So you know that I know."

Damn this woman! "Okay," I said, "I read it, and it looks like you correctly guessed some stuff about me."

"Correctly guessed," she said. "You always did have a way with words."

I could feel myself beginning to stutter, "I mean . . . I mean . . . You know . . ."

She cut me off, "You are the single most dangerous motherfucker on the face of the planet. Did you know that?"

Now, even my stuttering broke down, "Um . . . Uh . . ."

"Um, uh, nothing," she said, "if everybody in the world were like you, society would crumble."

I finally found my tongue. "But everybody in the world is *not* like me."

"That's right," she said. "That's what makes you dangerous."

"But you don't know me," I protested.

"Maybe *you* don't know you, but I damn well do. I saw you clear as crystal one night many years ago. Or have you forgotten that? The knowledge of who you are cost me my child. *Our* child."

I needed to change the subject. "Look," I said, "I'm not convinced that Benjamin is who you say he is."

"Fair enough," she answered. "I'll prove it. Who got this country into the Iraq war?"

"The folks who bombed the twin towers," I said.

"Okay, who bombed the twin towers?"

I didn't want to play a guessing game. "Tell me," I said.

"It was Benjamin."

"Aw, come on!"

Just then, she stopped. "Look," she said, "I'll give it to you straight."

"Thank you," I said.

"Benjamin needs to be killed because he killed America."

I had the strangest image of a pasty-faced Uncle Sam gasping for air, clutching at his collar with desperate fingers, sweat popping from his brow, his eyes bulging, knees buckling, his red, white and blue top hat careening to the ground. I couldn't resist the urge to chuckle.

"What about the Antichrist argument?"

"Bombing the Twin Towers was his inaugural Antichrist act. If we don't stop him, this country and the rest of the world will be awash in blood," she said. "It started with TWA flight 800," she continued.

"What?!"

"Let me finish."

"What has TWA got to do with the twin towers bombing?"

"It has everything to do with it," she said. "TWA flight 800 was the beginning of the death of American democracy."

"I know about TWA flight 800," I insisted.

"So, you know that the government is lying to the people about what happened there."

"Yes," I insisted again.

"But do you know *why* they are lying?"

I had to admit to myself that I was stumped. But since I didn't want Ida to know I was stumped, I began to ad-lib. "They wanted to save the airline industry," I asserted.

"Wrong," she said. "That's the lie they told us."

"What was the real reason?" I asked.

"They wanted to perpetuate the notion that this country is invulnerable, and that we don't make mistakes."

"What's that got to do with the twin towers?"

"Everything" she said, her voice rising with emphasis. "TWA flight 800 was the *second* terrorist attack on this country. It occurred in July of 1996. The first attack was the World Trade Center attack of February, 1993."

"And?" I asked.

"And to admit that flight 800 was another terrorist attack would be to admit that this country could be hit at any time. *That* would be a clear psychological victory for the jihad."

"Okay," I said, "the United States has been placated again. So now what?"

"So now, in steps Benjamin, the Antichrist. He meets with the U.S. president and vice-president in some small town in Texas. He convinces them that the only way to truly stop any more attacks on the U.S. is to go to war in the Middle East. Bear in mind," she continued, "it is not in Israel's best interest to have the U.S. on the sidelines in this matter. Israel *wants* the jihad to have that psychological victory. It is that psychological victory that would be used by Israel to spur the United States into war in the Middle East."

"But the jihad didn't make any more attacks," I said.

"Bingo!" she exclaimed. "So Benjamin had Israel make one on their behalf."

"On their behalf?" I chortled at the notion of Israel doing *anything* for the Arabs.

"It's called a false flag attack. Just like the one they did on the U.S.S.

Liberty, only bigger. This time, they killed two thousand American civilians."

"But why would our government buy into the scheme?" I was truly confused.

"Because now we don't have to wait for another TWA flight 800 that we would have to lie to cover up. Now we have the excuse to become pro-active. Hence, the War on Terror. Remember? That's when all this madness started. That's when American democracy began to convulse."

"Maybe you need to explain," I said.

"People in this country need to start thinking more like Timothy McVeigh," she answered.

"Timothy McVeigh?! What has *he* got to do with all this?"

"Timothy McVeigh!" she said. "Thank *God* for Timothy McVeigh! There was a true patriot. He set for himself a job, to strike a blow for freedom. It was a tough job, a job that he knew would cost him his life. But he didn't turn his back. He didn't ask, why me? He didn't look for someone else to do it. He did what he had to do! Just like Jesus did! Now, that took balls. That took conviction. Jesus whipped the money changers from the temple, and gave his life to save mankind. McVeigh blew the fuck out of the Murrah Building."

"McVeigh didn't know what he was doing," I said.

"McVeigh knew *exactly* what he was doing," she countered. "The government wants people to think McVeigh was a coward because he killed some kids, but he didn't know the kids were there. He did it in retaliation for what the government did at Waco. At Waco, the government killed the kids that it *knew* were there. It burned them alive. It burned them like hotdogs over a camp fire. Or shot them with automatic weapons if they tried to escape the flames. It sent armor-clad commandos into a nursery to do combat. How much bravery does *that* take?"

"Maybe they were only doing their jobs."

Again, she was on a roll, and not hearing much of what I had to say.

"McVeigh knew the truth! The biggest terrorist and rogue states in the world today are the United States of America, and its partner in crime, Israel. And exactly three months after his execution on June 11, 2001, they proved him correct. America launched its attack against the American people on September 11, 2001."

I knew better by now than to even attempt to stop her diatribe.

"Using Mossad agents who planted demolition explosives in World Trade Towers one, two and seven, it killed over 2,000 of its own citizens that day, blamed the attack on Osama Bin Laden, then used that blame to justify an attack on freedom and liberty worldwide. This false-flag attack was way more effective than the Israeli attack on the U.S.S. Liberty ever would have been. After the World Trade Center bombings, the U.S. attacked Afghanistan and Iraq. It drew up plans to attack Iran. It had the military divide the world into commands, and assigned a general to prepare plans for conquering the sector under each command. Intelligence was gathered on all the major cities in each command down to the smallest political subdivision. Data were gathered on the political beliefs of each person in each of the subdivisions. This country stands ready to attack any country anywhere on earth at any time. Under the guise of fighting terrorism, America is stomping out freedom around the globe."

I imagined a resurrected pasty-faced Uncle Sam crunching people under his boots while trying to recover his top hat.

"America is playing the name game," she continued. "It is changing the lexicon of democracy. American-sponsored terrorism is patriotism.

In-country patriots are gunmen or insurgents. Anyone opposing U.S. policy is considered a common criminal. In this new-world-order lexicon, up is down, and down is up. Fewer civil liberties make us 'free' from terror. More civil liberties endanger our security. Slavery is freedom!"

"Isn't that something Ayn Rand had one of her characters say?" I asked.

"I don't remember," she answered. "But if she did, that character was right. The in-country populations of countries around the world will be dehumanized. They will be given names that demean them and minimize their value. If they have no value, they are easy to kill. Past examples are gooks and hajjis."

Then, as if she suddenly remembered I was there, she looked at me.

"We mustn't play the game!" she said. "We must demand freedom whatever the cost. People in this country today are pussies! They think freedom is free. Well, it ain't. Freedom is purchased with blood, one drop at a time, one man at a time. McVeigh was such a man. He gave the last ounce, the last measure. Thank God for Timothy McVeigh!"

"If he was so good," I asked, "how come he got caught?"

I knew it was a bullshit question, but I wanted to get something in edgewise.

"McVeigh made two mistakes," she answered. "Number one, he didn't act alone. Bringing in another person is a sure-fire prescription for failure. The revolutionary can't control what other people do, and he can never be certain that the other person is as dedicated as he is. It's a hard and lonely lesson, but one that every revolutionary must learn. We should always act alone. Besides, acting alone prevents the creation of any tell-tale evidence of a conspiracy that the government might detect in advance. The larger the group, the more likely the FBI will be able to infiltrate and disrupt. The revolutionary mustn't forget the lessons to be learned from the U.S. government's handling of the Black Panther Party. Stay concealed. To expose oneself as a revolutionary soldier is to expose oneself to death.

"His second mistake was that he left too broad a trail. The truck, the fertilizer, the room, all traceable back to him. In the days to come, the war against tyranny will often require that the revolutionary rely on happenstance. Opportunities arise daily for one to gather materials for upcoming operations. Take advantage of them! Be vigilant and ever alert. Sometimes, supplies will present themselves at a time when their immediate use is as yet unknown. Be patient. The plan and the wherewithal to execute it will be presented at the exact right time.

"Finally, the revolutionary warrior must prepare himself. Study tactics. Study guerilla warfare. Study the techniques of the patriots in Algeria, Viet Nam, Afghanistan during the Russian invasion, and Iraq against the United States. All of these theaters, and others, will supply examples of tactics that will be useful when this government makes its move against the American people. For example, the improvised explosive devices used in Iraq can be used in an inner city conflict against the police with the same effectiveness."

"You really think it will come to that?" I asked.

"Yes," she answered. "It will come to exactly that. Waco and Ruby Ridge were training missions for the government. As if it were a giant game of chess, the government is positioning its pieces to put the people in check. And, as in any chess game, the positioning strategy must be executed stealthily. Most of the people in this country don't see it for what it is: the laws reducing our freedoms, the ever increasing power in the hands of law enforcement, the secret surveillance. But make no mistake about it, the war against terror is a war against the

American people.

"This is a battle for hearts and minds. There is no victory unless and until the hearts and minds are won. If those are won, there is no defeat. The revolutionary must always keep faith in the tactic, and never, ever fall for the rhetoric that attempts to define him as merely a gunman or an insurgent. He is a revolutionary and a patriot. And through his efforts, and the efforts of other fearless souls like him, America will be free again."

"Everybody has seen the films about the 911 attack," I said.

"Yes," she said, "we've all seen them. Yet, the current and past presidents, vice-presidents, and secretaries of state continue to perpetuate the ridiculous notion that a truth commission is needed to finally clear up the 911 conspiracy myth. Mind you, they have no intention of doing an actual investigation. They're not going to dig up ground zero looking for evidence. Because if they did, they would find evidence that explosives were used to bring the buildings down. Instead, they're merely going to issue a pronouncement that the Arabs did it, and continue with the War on Terror."

"Business as usual," I said.

"Exactly. And in time, the American people will come to believe the lie." She paused for a long moment. "That's where we come in."

"We?! What we?"

"You and me," she answered, "just like before."

"No," I said, "no, hell no."

She affected a sweet tone to her voice. "But why not, . . . What's your name now? Jay? But why not, Jay?"

"First off, I haven't agreed to do it. But secondly, I work alone these days. Just like you just said. You would only be in the way. And the last job we did together drove you crazy."

"Yeah, it did, didn't it?" She chuckled at herself. Then she got serious. "But this is too big for you to do alone."

"Then it won't get done."

"It *must* get done. Nathan Benjamin must die."

"He's only one man," I said.

"He is the Antichrist for Christ's sake!" She stood up abruptly, and said, "You're a punk, Al! You are a spineless asshole! When are you going to get some balls?"

"The name is Jay."

"Whatever!" She said, "It's just like before. You wouldn't join the Legion until our friends got killed. Well, what will it be this time? Who has to die, Al? Who has to die? I've got to go!"

She gathered up her things, and put her shoes back on. After getting out of the bathroom, she had taken them off and made herself at home. I guess now she was thinking that had been a mistake. Now, she could scarcely leave fast enough. She made her way to the door, and let herself out.

I sat quietly, and finished my tea.

I pulled out the 'My Life' sheet, and I stared at the blue numeral one with the blue period placed carefully behind it. I knew my first entry. I guessed I'd known it all along, but I didn't want to write it down. Writing something down was like bragging, or maybe 'confessing' was a better word. Either way, it was done. It was what I was sent to do, and I did it. I also now knew that the first entry is the only entry I needed to make. If the entry was a good one, it'd be the only one necessary. Mine was a good one.

I pulled out my pen. I felt almost regal as I unscrewed the cap and placed the nib on the paper. I made a stroke, but no ink appeared. That was okay, I was prepared. Reaching into my briefcase for another pen, I pricked my finger on the pin of a campaign button I had left in there. I flinched and snatched my hand from the bag. I squeezed the finger tip to see how bad the prick was, and a bubble of blood blossomed. I reached for a tissue, then stopped. I reached instead for my pen, and put the nib in the blood blossom. The nib sucked up the blood. I placed the nib on the bright white paper, and in bright red letters behind the blue numeral one, I wrote, "I killed Avel." I thought about it, then wrote it again behind the blue numeral two. I wrote it again and again and again. All of my hits were Avel over and over and over again. I filled the page with all the Avels I had hit over the years, the last one being the one I had just done in Texas. Corporate America would never be the same again.

I framed 'My Life', and mounted it on the wall over the fish tank. I rarely had company, but if I did, the first thing they would see as they walked into my apartment was the wall mounting of my life. It was there; it was complete. I read the entries again, and smiled. "I killed Avel." I felt so accomplished.

But what is 'accomplished?' What is success? And how should it *really* be measured? The universe is huge, and the universe is infinitesimal. Everything we do affects something on levels we cannot or will not or do not imagine. We arrange and rearrange atoms and molecules and cells; we kill and birth organisms large and small; we move the earth, plumb the seas, explore the heavens. But are we successful?

Maybe there is no success or failure. Maybe there is only *is*, being, existence. Maybe all one can do is what one does. Success and failure are irrelevant. Irrelevant because they are both temporary and temporal. Neither ever lasts. Both are short-lived, and neither requires the knowledge or acknowledgment of the actor. Was Van Gogh a success?

A failure? Both? Neither? Or was Van Gogh simply Van Gogh? He was who he was, and he did what he did. Then, after the fact, we imposed the attributes of success or failure.

The key is to live without imposing attributes. *That* is the magic of 'I am that I am.' There is no 'I am man,' or 'I am artist,' or 'I am good.' Any 'I am' other than 'I am' imposes an attribute that is temporary, temporal and irrelevant. Only 'I am' stands alone. Only 'I am' is timeless. Only 'I am' has meaning.

I wished Ida hadn't left. I wanted to tell her that it was okay what she did, what *we* did. Our actions, as do all actions, stand alone. Without preamble. Without apology. Without explanation. Any preamble, any apology, any explanation would be irrelevant. They would be attributes piled upon attributes. I wanted to tell her that she didn't have to be crazy. She didn't have to be sorry. She didn't have to explain.

Then I saw it. *She* didn't have to explain, but neither did *I*. Ida was, and Ida is. I was, and I am. No explanation was needed. So I stood up and fixed another cup of tea. I put water in the glass kettle with the black handle. I put the kettle on the stove, and adjusted a medium blue flame under it. While the water warmed, I looked through my selection of teas. I had green tea. I had peppermint. I had sassafras. I took one peppermint bag and one sassafras bag and put them in a fresh cup, a black cup with a yellow happy face on it. I poured the water, and dunked the bags. I put in a long squirt of honey, and stirred it up. I picked the cup up by the handle, and lifted it to my lips. I blew gently at the edge of the steaming liquid, and just as I was about to take a sip, the handle snapped. Hot tea spilled down the front of my clothes with the lion share landing in my lap and soaking my jeans. I lurched up from my chair as the cup slammed to the floor and shattered.

XX

"Which hand do you jack-off with?"

I didn't know how to answer. I certainly didn't want to say the left. That would have been true, but I didn't want to have to admit that I had ever jacked-off at all. I was instantly so determined to lie, that I almost said the right. Granted, that would have been a lie, but it wouldn't have resolved my quandary. Instead, I began to mumble something about not doing that kind of thing. Just then, my questioner saved me.

"Hey, man," he said, "we all do it." He was gesturing to the half dozen or so guys sitting around him. "I use my left," he continued. "Moo-Moo over there," he pointed to a light-skinned boy with freckles on his cheeks and nose, "he uses his right. I did it this morning before coming to school. I couldn't help it."

Everybody there laughed. I stifled mine, but a smile leaked out anyway.

It was warm out, and I was in the park across from Hyde Park High earlier than usual. I hadn't done my math homework, so I cut class. Now I was walking around aimlessly waiting for my usual partners to themselves come to lunch.

"I'm Pookey. This Joe. You know Moo-Moo."

I gave them my first name. I wasn't sure yet that I wanted them to have my family name.

"Here," Pookey said, "sit with us for a minute."

I was nervous, but I tried to act cool and relaxed as I sat in the grass at the edge of the collective.

Pookey was a big, round shouldered guy with a scar shaped like a 'C' in the middle of his dark and sloped and shiny forehead.

"So which hand you use?" Moo-Moo asked, his voice squawked like an old radio.

Somehow, answering him wasn't as intimidating as answering Pookey. "I use them both," I said. "Sometimes one, sometimes the other, sometimes both at the same time."

Now they laughed for real. "Yeah, me, too," Joe said. He was a skinny boy with big feet and a face full of acne pimples.

"Sometimes that shit be better than pussy," Pookey said. "And it's always there." He laughed at himself, hunching his shoulders with each hoot.

I still didn't want to do a full laugh like everybody else, but I couldn't stop the sharp gusts escaping from my nose. Maybe these guys weren't so bad.

Just then, I saw Puck across the street. He was sitting on the concrete apron around the school lawn. While Pookey and the guys giggled about self-induced orgasms, I was transfixed staring at Puck who was absorbed in some book he was reading. He was alone. His girlfriends were nowhere to be seen. And it wasn't so much Puck that held my attention. Rather, it was the book he was reading. I couldn't see the title from that distance, but I could see the color of the cover. It was an odd mustard yellow. And the reason that it caught my attention was that I had only seen one book in my life with a cover that color. The book was one I had seen on the coffee table in my livingroom about a year earlier. It was a book that Grandma Daughter had left there for me to find. It was the book that had information about the Egyptian Sphinx that I had never seen before. It was the book that had the quaternary of the magi, and I was consumed with the notion that Puck knew what Grandma Daughter knew.

Then I dismissed it. How could it possibly be that it was the same book? I was too far away to see the title. Lots of books probably had that same color. And maybe the color I was remembering was wrong. Maybe I didn't really get a good look at the cover.

Pookey nudged me.

"Hey, Man," he said, "don't be getting so deep on us. Deep thought can be a dangerous thing."

"I got to go," I said. I stood up, and headed for the main entrance to the school.

XXI

I had another dream. This time, I was a four year old white boy. I don't know how it came to pass that a white boy had black parents, but dreams are like that.

Mama was a loving mother, so she wasn't in the dream much. I just kind of knew she was there. It was daddy's images that predominated. And the one image that dominated most was one of disgust. That was the expression he wore whenever he looked at me. It isn't clear if I disgusted him because I was white, or if I disgusted him because I was weak and inept, and I was using being white as some kind of rationale to make it look as if his expression were unwarranted.

The thing was, I didn't really remember a lot about my father. So, I couldn't even imagine what the dream meant. I knew he was a steel worker. I knew he got sick and died shortly after Grandma Daughter came and lived with us. I knew he used to beat my mother, but that she loved him anyway. I knew she used to tell me stories about him and how they used to be so much in love. But none of these would account for me dreaming about him now at my advanced age. In fact, I've hardly thought about the man in years, decades actually.

In the dream, everything I did was to get his approval. The dream wasn't specific about what I did, but being that I was only four years old, it couldn't have been much. Maybe that was the issue. Maybe I was not trying enough things. Maybe his expectations of a four-year-old were exaggerated. It really wasn't clear.

I remembered one thing about him. I remembered that he drank a lot. I remembered that he accused Grandma Daughter of turning his wife against him. And thinking back, that look of disgust was the same one he used to give to her. The day she stepped off the City of New

Orleans at the Illinois Central station at 63rd Street, he had that look of disgust on his face. And as I thought about it, I must have been around three or four years old at the time.

I wanted to make some kind of connection between my age in the dream and my age when Grandma Daughter came to live with us, or between daddy giving that look of disgust to me in my dream, and to Grandma Daughter when she first arrived in Chicago, but all the connections I could think of seemed to defy logic. I struggled to make the connection, because, in my mind, making a connection would be the same as having an epiphany. Making a connection would reveal to me some secret that I was longing to uncover.

I struggled to see my father's face in the dream. He was light-skinned. High yellow we used to call it. He was a tall, muscular man with a big lumberjack's neck. Whenever he turned his head, the muscles in his neck stood out like heavy ropes. His Adam's apple protruded like a sparrow's head caught in his throat, and it bobbed up and down whenever he talked or swallowed. His big neck made his head look small. A lot of people thought he was good-looking because he had curly hair that was almost auburn, and almond-colored eyes. And with his small, turned-up nose and thin lips, he looked almost like a white man.

His hands were big, too, big and knobby. The skin on them was rough and chapped and callused. The first phalanx on each of his fingers and thumbs was thicker than the other phalanges so that his fingers looked like a collection of little mallets or pendulums. His fingernails were like little, flat plastic shields, chipped and broken and dirty around the edges. The nail on the index finger of his left hand was purple from where he had hit it with a hammer.

Try as I might, though, I couldn't make the connection I sought.

The fact that some of my facial features were similar to those of Grandma Daughter's, and the fact that Daddy gave both of us the same look of disgust, meant nothing. I woke up feeling empty and drained and curiously nostalgic. I got up and brushed my teeth and took a shower. I guess I was hoping that starting the day would rid me of the off-kilter feeling that dream had left me with. It didn't work. By the time I was half way through my oatmeal, I had to get up from the table, and go look for some old pictures I knew I had around the house somewhere.

I kept a collection of pictures in shoe boxes on the top shelf of my closet. I had other pictures strewn in my desk and chest of drawers, but I felt drawn to the shoe boxes. I took them down, three of them. The first one had nothing except snapshots of some of the places I had visited while working on various contracts, sites around Cleveland, New York, Houston, Portland, Maine and Portland, Oregon, Los Angeles. For obvious reasons, I never made any more hits in Chicago. The second box held more of the same. The third box held the charm. That's where I found an old picture of Grandma Daughter someone had taken with a Brownie box camera the day of Daddy's funeral. The sky that day was overcast and grey.

I held the picture in front of me. Looking at it caused a flood of memories to return. She came to live with us right after my grandfather, Paw-paw, got killed in an accident at a sawmill in Memphis, Tennessee. My remembrances of her were and still are divided into two categories. The first category contains images of her working around the kitchen in blue flannel house slippers that slapped the bottoms of her feet as she walked, and of her stirring cornbread batter with a big wooden spoon as sweat beaded on her nose and the batter clapped together with a muffled thud.

Grandma Daughter moved more gracefully than her size would suggest. Her calves were thick boles of flesh, and her buttocks rose up on each side like bags of laundry strapped around her waist. She walked, however, like a much lighter woman. In fact, she walked on the balls of her feet with a deliberate controlled rhythm, like a dancer.

She was as dark as molasses. The skin on her face was soft and smooth and downy like rich, brown velvet, and as a young boy, I liked it whenever she rubbed her face against mine. Sometimes she would kiss me all over my face. And I would get so excited, I would hug her around her neck as hard as I could. Then she would hold me away from her and look at me. And I would look at her. And her eyes were dark brown and fluid as she narrowed them slightly when she smiled at me. They were bottomless and mysterious like a crystal ball resting on deep brown velvet. I used to stare at her face, up close, and just look into her eyes trying to see what was in them. I asked her once, "Grandma Daughter, what's in your eyes?"

"You are," she answered.

I looked closely, and sure enough, my reflection was there. But there was more. Deep down there was much more. Grandma Daughter had the kind of eyes that were not afraid to look at people. Her eyes held power. Their movements were steady and deliberate. And most people who looked her in the eye looked away after only a few moments. If she were mad at me, she could make me tingle with fear simply by staring at me. And after seeing me hurt, she could soothe me long before she was close enough to touch me. I never told her what I saw in her eyes, but as I looked at the rest of her face with its shiny cheeks, its long, angular nose and flaring nostrils, its wide, thick lips that turned up slightly at the corners with an inborn smile, I suspected that she knew what was there.

The second category of remembrances is less lucid than the first. It is also the more interesting of the two. The images in this second category are only half-images, though, the result of glimpses of Grandma Daughter crying at times as she read the Bible, and smiling an almost wicked smile at other times as she read it. Whenever she caught me watching her, she would either close the book or tell me a story about the life of Jesus. I never knew which she would do, and whichever one she selected always surprised me because invariably I had guessed the other. These images are of her burning candles and incense, and making a series of strange hand gestures as an ambulance or fire truck would roar by. It was like Catholics crossing themselves, but different. She would put the palm of her right hand to her forehead, then to her heart, then to her navel. She would say that the noise upset her stomach and gave her a headache, but I knew it wasn't true because the noise never bothered anybody else. In fact, nobody else would even notice the noise if the sirens were at a distance. But Grandma Daughter always heard them and always palmed herself. She later told me she palmed herself to acknowledge God's intervention on Earth.

It was Grandma Daughter who set me on my current career path. It was she who killed my father! He didn't simply get sick. Grandma Daughter cursed him, and he died. Her solution to the problem of my father beating her and my mother was to kill him.

It worked. We lived a good life after he was gone. I couldn't help but wonder, though, whether or not she saw in me the creature I now know she had to have known was in herself. Oh, she used an intermediary and magic to kill my father, but kill him she did. She watched him suffer with headaches for months. When he died, she smiled, and picked up her Bible.

I looked at the back of the picture I was holding. I was hoping to see someone's name or a date or some written message saying something, anything. It was blank. I looked at her image again more closely. I looked at the expression on her face. I looked at her eyes. And I don't know if it was something I actually saw, or something I remembered and thought I saw, or what, but suddenly I knew Grandma Daughter like I had never known her when she was alive. She was the personification of power. She could heal or she could kill; she could live or she could die. It was all the same. And in her, I saw me. In that instant, I knew that I, too, was the personification of power. There was nothing in the universe that I could not do. Men's laws did not apply to her, and they did not apply to me. The discomfort my dream had left me with melted away. I could feel the calm soothing every cell of my body.

I stacked the boxes back in the closet, and finished eating my cereal.

Later, I walked over to the computer and logged onto Travelocity.com. I typed 'Chicago' in the 'From' box. In the 'To' box, I typed 'Tel Aviv.'

About the author

Larry Redmond is a writer, photographer and attorney. He attended the University of Illinois at Chicago, where he majored in Philosophy and minored in English. He later attended the John Marshall Law School, earning a Juris Doctor degree. He has worked as a criminal defense attorney representing high-profile death row inmates, several of whom were released pursuant to DNA testing. He is a member of the National Lawyers Guild.

Larry Redmond is a member of the Perspectivists writers collective, the oldest continuously active writers' workshop in Chicago.

He studied Art and Photography at Chicago State University, and became a member of the Chicago Alliance of African-American Photographers. He is also a member of the Washington Park Camera Club, one of the oldest continuously running camera clubs in Chicago.

He has seven children and two grandchildren. His hobbies include physical training and martial arts, and yoga and meditation.

He currently works and lives with his family in Chicago, Illinois.

Visit Penknife Press, the quill that can cut you, on-line at

www.penknifepress.com.